Nihilist Girl

SOFYA KOVALEVSKAYA

Nihilist Girl

Translated by
Natasha Kolchevska
with Mary Zirin

Introduction by
Natasha Kolchevska

The Modern Language Association of America
New York   2001

To order MLA publications, visit www.mla.org/books. For wholesale and
international orders, see www.mla.org/bookstore-orders.

The MLA office is located on the island known as Mannahatta
(Manhattan) in Lenapehoking, the homeland of the Lenape people. The
MLA pays respect to the original stewards of this land and to the diverse
and vibrant Native communities that continue to thrive in New York City.

Cover illustration: *Kursistka* (Woman College Student), 1881, by Nikolai
Yaroshenko (1846–98). Courtesy of the Kaluga Regional Art Museum

Texts and Translations 8
ISSN 1079-2538

POD 2022 (fifth printing)

Library of Congress Cataloging-in-Publication Data

Kovalevskaia, S.V. (Sof ia Vasil evna), 1850–1891.
[Nigilistka. English]
Nihilist girl / Sofya Kovalevskaya; translated by Natasha Kolchevska with
    Mary Zirin ; introduction by Natasha Kolchevska.
p. cm. — (Texts and translations. Translations ISSN 1079-2538; 8)
Includes bibliographical references.
ISBN-13: 978-0-87352-790-3 (pbk.)
I. Kolchevska, Natasha. II. Title. III. Series.
    PG3467.K637 N513 2001
891.73'3—dc21   2001030985

TABLE OF CONTENTS

ACKNOWLEDGMENTS

First and foremost, I would like to thank Mary F. Zirin, who served invaluably as reader and critic. I would also like to thank my student Joan Saberhagen, who first brought Kovalevskaya's literary work to my attention, and to Michael Katz, for graciously suggesting that I submit *Нигилистка* to the MLA Texts and Translations series. Susanne Baackmann, Melissa Bokovoy, Ann Hibner Koblitz, Lorraine Piroux, and Jane Slaughter helped me turn earlier drafts of the introduction into a readable essay that contextualizes Kovalevskaya's novella. Thanks also to Dilyara Doyanova for her proofreading of the Russian annotations and to Vladimir Chudnov for his help in obtaining the right to reproduce N. Yaroshenko's painting on the cover of this book. Finally, I would like to thank the editor of the MLA Texts and Translation series, Martha Evans, for her unflagging support; Michael Kandel, the MLA's excellent copy editor, for his many stylistic suggestions; the editorial board for their confidence in me; and the anonymous readers for their helpful and knowledgeable comments.

INTRODUCTION

Background

The life, career, and writings of Sofya Vasilevna Kovalevskaya (born Sofya Korvin-Krukovskaya in 1850, died 1891), the author of *Nihilist Girl*, exemplify many of the hopes and disappointments of Russians of her generation, her class, and her gender. She was born into a family of landed nobility (gentry) on the eve of the period in Russian history known as the era of great reforms, which lasted from the end of the Crimean War and Tsar Nicholas I's death in 1855 until Alexander II's assassination in 1881. Kovalevskaya was simultaneously a product of her milieu, a beneficiary of the greater opportunities that opened up for women, and a casualty of the often unsatisfactory nature of those opportunities. She was a pioneering mathematician whose achievements were widely acclaimed throughout Europe and Russia long before her death at the age of forty-one. Yet the obstacles that this talented and driven woman faced in both her professional and private lives reveal the complexities women faced when entering traditionally male-dominated institutions during the second half of the nineteenth century in Russia and western Europe. Kovalevskaya's turn late in her short life to literary pursuits similarly underlines the importance of two other interests that played an important role in her life as well as in the lives of many men and women of her generation: the commitment to social activism and self-determination for women and the belief in literature as an explicator and essential "guide to life," in the formulation of the major driving force behind that view, Nikolay Chernyshevsky (see Paperno, esp. ch. 1).

In a comprehensive biography of Kovalevskaya, Ann Hibner Koblitz sees in her subject a unique "convergence of lives"—scientific, social, and literary—but the notion of convergence can be broadly applied to the whole generation of Russian women and men who matured in the 1860s. These children of the sixties integrated and expanded the changes initiated by Alexander II into something that was less a cohesive political program than a cultural ethos for their generation, a collection of practices that served as much as a mode of self-definition as it did as a means to redress Russia's social ills and material backwardness. Unlike the more philosophically and aesthetically oriented idealists of the previous generation of Russian intelligentsia, Kovalevskaya's peers were not content merely to chronicle and analyze those ills. Rather, they sought to create a new culture that would result in major, wide-ranging changes in the life of Russia's long-neglected underclasses— the peasants and increasingly, by the 1880s, the urban working class. While a repeated and widely articulated goal for Kovalevskaya's generation was the formation of a more representative and civic-minded society in the period following the emancipation of the serfs in 1861, there was also a more radical component to this ethos. Not unlike the avant-garde left in postrevolutionary Russia (or their

American analogues in the 1960s), Russia's nihilists, as they came to be called by the early 1860s, wanted no less than the transformation of all aspects of life, from political institutions to domestic relations and customs to modes of dress and behavior.

As the two generational antipodes Pavel Kirsanov (1840s) and Evgeny Bazarov (1860s) illustrate so tellingly in Ivan Turgenev's *Fathers and Sons*, one of the defining novels of the period, education was no longer viewed as an adjunct to gentility or good breeding or as a vehicle of moral indoctrination; instead it was seen as a tool for creating activists who would lead the fight to improve the plight of the masses. It is no accident that Turgenev made Bazarov a doctor, for the intellectual explosion of the 1860s focused on the natural sciences as the dominant paradigm for intellectual endeavor. Such men and women of education and action would serve Russia most effectively as it moved toward reform and progress. In the minds of Kovalevskaya's generation, Russia's future would be driven by its scientific achievements. Young Russians, no longer only from the gentry and aristocracy, streamed to natural science curricula in Russian universities and dominated the press with their positivist, empiricist, and scientist writings. Intellectuals' preoccupation with science did not appear in a vacuum. Acknowledging that the national shame of losing the Crimean War had been caused by Russia's technological disadvantages, the tsarist government made scientific education a priority beginning with the secondary schools. The early years of Alexander II's reign saw an enormous expansion of both university facilities and curricula.

New disciplines were introduced into the course of study, a post-graduate system was initiated in 1863, laboratories were founded, research institutes flourished, and tremendous advances were made in the biological sciences, especially physiology [. . .], in mathematics [. . .], in chemistry [. . .], and in the earth sciences like geology [. . .]. In this climate of discovery and possibility, science was not the only source of enlightenment, but it was regarded as the highest form of intellectual accomplishment, as Russia celebrated what it needed and was beginning to know.

(McReynolds and Popkin 82–83)

The government's drive to expand higher education and open it to larger segments of the Russian population was extended to women only reluctantly and erratically, however. Despite initial attempts in the late 1850s to allow women to matriculate in institutions of higher education, as the ties between greater educational opportunities for women and social activism became apparent and therefore threatening to the authorities, a decree was issued in 1863 specifically barring women from attending such institutions. It was not until the early 1870s that parallel institutions known as Higher Courses of Education for Women appeared, but even into the 1880s their existence was tenuous and they were often subject to government closure. Before that time, women impatient for the prospects of a higher education went abroad, most often to Switzerland or Germany, to pursue a university education. In the 1860s, these were well-off women from the gentry, which constituted only three percent of Russia's population at the time. Since unmarried Russian women could not obtain passports for travel abroad, the "fictitious marriage," based on a mutual bond not of love but of shared dedication to improving women's access to education, was born. Sofya Korvin-Krukovskaya was among the first to avail herself of that ruse, finding a spiritual brother, a young paleontologist and supporter of women's right to self-determination, Vladimir Kovalevsky, to marry her. Over her parents' strenuous objections, the couple married in 1868 and left soon thereafter for Heidelberg. Initially, Sofya Kovalevskaya intended to study medicine but soon switched to mathematics.

Throughout the second half of the nineteenth century, there were two main, often overlapping forums for social, literary, and political discourse in Russian public life. One was the "thick journal," a uniquely Russian form that combined literature, literary criticism, social commentary, and articles on the natural sciences; it attracted some of Russia's greatest writers and social thinkers to its pages as contributors and readers. The second was the Russian realist novel, and to a lesser extent its shorter variant, the novella. Both genres were often first published in thick journals, and this configuration of forum and genre allowed the realist novel and novella to take the lead in reconfiguring the writer's role with respect to society in late empire Russia. Beginning with Turgenev's *Fathers and Sons* (published in 1862) and Chernyshevsky's *What Is to Be Done?* (published one year later), not only the novel but the author himself (and it was predominantly male authors) came to play a far more significant role in determining the major discourses of Russian public life. As Irina Paperno describes in her study of Chernyshevsky's impact, for writers and other potential leaders in the transformation of Russia's social consciousness, "this role entailed a deliberate psychological self-organization in which one's private personality, one's psychic life itself, was shaped to conform to a historical mold. For Chernyshevsky, this was an essential, if not the most important, part of the vocation of the writer" (37–38).

In their heyday, from 1860 to 1880, the novel and the novella took the lead in provoking debate and molding the contours of public opinion on myriad social issues. Not the least of these concerned the role of women in public as well as domestic life. Literature's place in these discussions was twofold: to represent life as realistically as possible but also to present readers with models for living that they would then incorporate into their own lives. Paperno observes that "the literary model possess[ed] a remarkable power to organize the actual life of the reader"(9). Russian culture had never had a strong inclination to allow writers to remain solely in the literary realm. Writers of every ideological bias, supported by their often eagerly complicit readers, imposed their authority on the world beyond the page, justifying such intrusions by citing the urgent need to correct Russia's backwardness. Moreover, this conflation of literature and life, of art and activism, often drove writers to dispense with the conventions governing literary genres, and many works of this period present heterogeneous amalgams of genres, languages, and styles whose literary merits are only now being acknowledged.[1]

Although she did not come to creative writing until the late 1880s, the author of *Nihilist Girl* (Kovalevskaya's only completed work of fiction) similarly puts her imagination, experience, and memory into concrete form by writing a tale that crosses generic and stylistic boundaries. Like other writers of her generation, she uses literary types to embody and explore potential ways of being and acting in the Russian context. In *Nihilist Girl*, Kovalevskaya brings together in hybridized fictional form autobiographical elements—details of her childhood, education, and social goals—and a character study of a socioliterary type, the idealistic young gentry woman who leaves behind the comforts of home and family to find autonomy and at the same time serve the radical cause. Cognizant of more than one variation on this type, Kovalevskaya splits her heroine into two figures, the narrator and the nihilist girl, to explore two generationally demarcated variations on her theme. The author thereby creates a narrative space to include a number of other discourses that testify to her own multiple positions in the text and the world. Kovalevskaya exists both as narrator of her imagined tale and as the renowned scientist and worldly woman who figures in this tale. By engaging with both worlds, the author-narrator establishes authority over her text while simultaneously exercising the right to incorporate any factual material she finds necessary for her narrative, and it is in this conjunction of document and fiction that the strength of her narrative lies.

Biography

There is little question that Sofya Kovalevskaya was one of the leading European intellectuals of her generation.[2] By the time of her death, she had left her mark in the public consciousness of Russia and Europe through a series of firsts. She and her friend Yulya Lermontova were among the first women to enroll at European universities (in Heidelberg); Kovalevskaya was the first European woman to receive a doctorate in mathematics, summa cum laude at the age of twenty-four, from the University of Göttingen. She was the first nineteenth-century European woman to hold a tenured teaching appointment in mathematics, at the University of Stockholm. She was also the first female member of the Russian Academy of Sciences.[3] From 1884, she was the first woman to serve on the editorial board of one of Europe's leading scientific journals, *Acta Mathematica*, and in 1888 she received the prestigious Bordin Prize from the French Academy for a groundbreaking solution to a problem in mathematical physics. These honors were insufficient, however, to secure for Kovalevskaya a university teaching position in Russia, where laws forbade women from teaching in higher educational institutions, including the Higher Courses of Education for Women in Saint Petersburg, where they could supervise laboratories or classrooms but were barred as regular faculty members. Frustrated by the barriers she repeatedly encountered when applying for university teaching positions, for a good part of the 1880s Kovalevskaya commuted between the academic worlds of western Europe and the urban salons and country estates of Russia. In 1883, she left Russia to assume a regular faculty position at the University of Stockholm. Toward the end of her years in Sweden, Kovalevskaya finally found a modicum of stability and peace and picked up the pen. In 1891, she died in Stockholm from complications of a bronchial infection.

Much of what we know about Kovalevskaya's childhood, her family, and her budding interest in mathematics, social justice, and literature comes from her childhood memoir, written in those last years. The memoir has been translated into English as *A Russian Childhood*. Born in Moscow into a prosperous and reasonably well educated gentry family, Kovalevskaya was the middle child of Lieutenant General Vasily Vasilevich Korvin-Krukovsky and Elizaveta Fyodorovna Shubert. Aware that the pending emancipation of the serfs would require a more active management of his properties, Kovalevskaya's father retired from active service in 1858 and moved the family to Palibino, the extensive family estate in western Russia. Kovalevskaya lived there until her departure for Europe in 1868, her winters typically spent in Saint Petersburg (spending the winter season in one of Russia's two "capitals," Moscow or Saint Petersburg, was considered de rigueur among prerevolutionary gentry families).

From an early age, Sofya Kovalevskaya showed a remarkable aptitude for mathematics: she recounts the first inkling of that talent—a temporary shortage of wallpaper for the walls of her nursery that forced the family to paper them with

> the lithographed lectures of Professor [Mikhail] Ostrogradsky on differential and integrated calculus. [. . .] These sheets, all speckled over with strange and unintelligible formulas, soon attracted my attention. I remember as a child standing for hours on end in front of this mysterious wall, trying to figure out at least some isolated sentences. (*Childhood* 122–23)

Initially, Kovalevskaya's conservative father was unwilling to allow his daughter to pursue formal studies in mathematics, but he relented after the evidence of his daughter's talents provided by a perceptive uncle and a dedicated tutor became overwhelming. The precocious mathematician's passion for her subject also played a role in swaying her authoritarian but, in her account, lovable father. As she breezily observes in recalling her family, "oftentimes the children reeducated the parents" (Koblitz 43).

In her memoir, Kovalevskaya traces both her commitment to social causes and her literary interests to the influence of her sister, Anyuta, seven years older, who had decided at an early age to become a revolutionary and a writer. By the age of twenty-one, Anyuta had published two stories in Fyodor Dostoevsky's thick journal, *Epoch*. Beyond an often intense but loving sibling rivalry and an early proclivity for storytelling, in their adult lives the two sisters shared a strong desire to liberate themselves from their comfortable, patriarchal family to pursue their educational and literary interests abroad and to identify more active roles for themselves in changing Russian society. It is unlikely that either one alone could have escaped from parental oppression. Together, in 1867, they began searching for suitable "suitors," that is, men who shared their commitment to women's rights and education. The younger sister's marriage in 1868 to Vladimir Kovalevsky enabled her not only to leave Russia to pursue her studies in Heidelberg but also, under the guise of familial devotion, to bring her sister to Europe as well.

Heidelberg was but the first stop in academic venues for Kovalevskaya over the next six years—Berlin and Zurich among them—both with and without her husband. As Sofya's letters to Vladimir vividly reveal, her marriage was initially based on ideological principles and later merged with more traditionally romantic ones. Unsatisfactory for both partners, it was a complicated affair. Sofya received her doctorate in 1874 but returned to Russia when neither she nor her husband could find academic positions abroad. The couple spent the next five years in Russia, jointly and independently pursuing a variety of academic and business enterprises, almost all of which came to naught, virtually her entire inheritance spent on one ill-considered, utopian business or journalistic enterprise after another. A daughter, also named Sofya, was born in 1878. Well-connected through her mother's family and her own undeniable achievements, Kovalevskaya moved easily through Saint Petersburg's and Moscow's literary and scientific salons. Nonetheless, she continued to search for a suitable position abroad. Although the Kovalevskys were never officially divorced, their marriage dissolved in early 1881. That same year, Sofya went to Berlin, to renew her work in mathematics after a seven-year hiatus in Russia. Two years later, her husband ran up major debts, was implicated in a major oil-company scandal, and committed suicide.

Thus, at the age of thirty-three, Sofya Kovalevskaya found herself a widow. Her new status was actually an improvement on her earlier ambiguous marriage, socially if not economically (since she had a five-year-old daughter to support). Also, she was finally a top candidate for a teaching position at the University of Stockholm. After six months as an untenured and unpaid privatdocent, in the summer of 1884 she was officially appointed professor of mathematics, the only woman in Europe to hold a university-level teaching post at that time. Despite the social and linguistic difficulties she experienced adjusting to her new life, the years she spent in Sweden were her most productive in terms of both professional and social recognition. Her ambition and talents, however, seemed to intimidate people wherever she lived—the Swedish playwright August Strindberg declared about Kovalevskaya that "a female professor [is] a monstrosity"(Koblitz 230). Strindberg's misogynistic dictum aside, she was comparatively well received in Stockholm's cultural and scientific circles. During the last two years of her life, Kovalevskaya cowrote a socially conscious play with Anna Carlotta Leffler, a Swedish friend and colleague. Just as during her formative years she had been deeply involved with many of Russia's leading intellectual and social pacesetters, she became acquainted with many of Sweden's writers at a period of rapid development for letters in that nation.

A combination of factors—the stability of a genuine academic position, her sister's death in 1887, the appearance of a new love in her life,[4] and, probably, most important, a need for social action (or was it self-examination?) that had been unfulfilled in the effort to establish herself in an academic career—brought Sofya to take up writing in 1888. The last three years of her life were the most productive for her literary creativity.

Nihilist Girl

At her death, Kovalevskaya left behind a relatively small body of literary and journalistic writings alongside the studies in theoretical mathematics for which she had become widely known throughout Europe in her lifetime.[5] An effective merging of creative impulse and social purpose, *Nihilist Girl* is the last and longest of her fictional works and the only one to be completed. The unusual conjunction of mathematics and literary interests appeared quite natural to Kovalevskaya, as she wrote to a friend in the fall of 1890:

> You are surprised at my working simultaneously in literature and in mathematics. Many people who have never had occasion to learn what mathematics is confuse it with arithmetic and consider it a dry and arid science. In actual fact, it is the science that demands the most imagination. One of the foremost mathematicians of our century says very justly that it is impossible to be a mathematician without also being a poet in spirit. It goes without saying that to understand

the truth of this statement one must repudiate the old prejudice by which poets are supposed to fabricate what does not exist and that imagination is the same as "making things up." It seems to me that the poet must see what others do not see, must see more deeply than other people.

(Vospominaniia i pis'ma 314; my trans.)

It is curious that the author of a work provocatively titled *Nihilist Girl* does not link her art with social action in this passage, especially since Kovalevskaya herself had a reputation as a nihilist. Indeed, she was turned down for a professorship at Helsinki University because of that reputation (Koblitz 155), and recent historians have characterized her as a "real-life example of a 'Bazarova,'" namely, a spiritual sister to Turgenev's nihilist hero, Bazarov (McReynolds and Popkin 82).

The figure of the nihilist plays a central role in post-emancipation intellectual Russian life and is a recurring type in the fiction of that period. The term had been in circulation earlier in the nineteenth century, but once Bazarov declared in *Fathers and Sons* that he believed in nothing (*nihil*), it became a widely (mis)used term for radicals of the 1860s. It is plausible that Kovalevskaya, familiar with the spin that journalists and writers of her generation had put on the figure of the nihilist, was seeking to illuminate the changing meanings of that term for younger radicals. Initially, it signified an aggregate of attitudes that had less to do with social transformation than with personal growth. Nihilists of the 1860s came from the well-educated members of the gentry, like Kovalevskaya, but also from the small but growing numbers of men and women of lesser ranks, the *raznochintsy*. Though of varying social backgrounds, this generation set out to educate itself (preferably in the sciences), to acquire the necessary tools to improve conditions of life and work in Russia, and thereby to create a critical mass of "critically thinking individuals," to borrow Abbott Gleason's phrase, who would take the lead role in defining and remedying Russia's ills. The emphasis, then, for this first generation of nihilists, was on individual growth and education. As Gleason has written in his study of Russian radicalism of this period, "Nihilist attitudes always involved a strong belief in the unfettering of the individual, a *personal* revolt against societal standards that were regarded as backward and oppressive" (71).

Thus the retrospective narrative of *Nihilist Girl* (written in 1890-91), which spans a period from the late 1850s to 1874, can be read as Kovalevskaya's attempt to recover and understand the often complex relationship of that first generation, the young men and women of the 1860s, with its successors. Although the narrator, who is easily identified with Kovalevskaya herself, is only slightly older than her heroine and although both come from similar backgrounds, they present two very different, generationally specific definitions of a nihilist. As the narrator's biography and life choices illustrate, her cohort was generally better off, more socially homogeneous, and more elitist than the men and women of the generation of Vera Barantsova, the protagonist.

The children of the 1860s had a keen desire to liberate themselves from familial, social, and cultural restraints—hence the push for formal education. And they felt that educated Russians had a good deal to learn from the West—hence the desire to travel and work abroad. Committed to social progress, they also believed in the freedom of a well-educated and necessarily small elite to discover and interpret intellectual truths for themselves. In turn, these individuals would be the leaders in championing the transformations that Russia desperately needed.

By contrast, as the trial scene in *Nihilist Girl* demonstrates so tellingly, the radicals who came of age in the 1870s were much more socially heterogeneous: this was, after all, the decade when the numbers and prominence in public life of *raznochintsy* rapidly increased. More inclined to search for concrete and direct ways of serving the people, Vera's generation, the self-styled populists of the 1870s, believed in the wisdom of the Russian peasants and native institutions as opposed to the scientific and philosophical positions imported from the West by Kovalevskaya's generation.[6] Through her preference for direct action and self-sacrifice over education and reformist political activity, as well as through her adoption of specific behaviors and patterns of dress and comportment, Vera exemplifies the practices and tendencies of this younger, populist version of the nihilist.

The gendered implications of Kovalevskaya's novella also need to be elucidated. One of the focal points of recent feminist scholarship has been to look at women authors' attempts to name—that is, to define—on their own terms women's culture and what was called the woman question (Costlow 62). Kovalevskaya, so active in defining her character and setting goals in her own life, shifts to a literary medium here, but her intentions remain the same. By focusing on a nihilist girl, she uses this gender label to explore and undermine the frequently held (in the conservative press and common usage), but in her opinion wildly mistaken, image of an unfeminine, intolerant, lascivious, and egotistical young woman who renounces domestic life for the public arena. Vera Barantsova deviates from that stereotype in many important details—physical, emotional, and behavioral—thereby refocusing the discourse to the complexities and difficulties of one of the most enduring literary and human paradigms: the search for self-definition and purpose in a chaotic and rapidly changing world.

Koblitz has observed that Kovalevskaya "was at her best when writing fictionalized accounts of events through which she had lived" (262), and it is the creative interweaving of autobiography and social history into fictional narrative that makes *Nihilist Girl* more than a work of historical interest. Her tale was based on an encounter with an actual person, Vera Sergeevna Goncharova, a niece of Alexandr Pushkin's wife, who married a student, a revolutionary, to whom she had been introduced by Kovalevskaya. Writing her novella some years later, the author was familiar with the outcome of Goncharova's true story, whose denouement was much less happy than the novella would suggest: the couple had left Russia illegally and were married in Paris, where Kovalevskaya found them, a tyrannical husband and an unhappy wife with a baby. The author provided Goncharova with money and a passport so that she could return to Russia. Subsequently, Kovalevskaya stood up to the husband's threat to throw acid in her face for helping the young woman.

In many instances, the account of Vera's childhood, which makes up the long middle section of the novella, draws on the author's early experiences. Kovalevskaya places generational conflict and the search for autonomy at the center of both her autobiography and *Nihilist Girl*, her two most accomplished narratives. Like Vera, Kovalevskaya grew up in a patriarchal family complete with English and French governesses, manorial homes, and connections in high places in Saint Petersburg and elsewhere.[7] Her father, like Vera's, was a retired lieutenant general, although scandal did not force him, as it did his fictionalized counterpart, to leave the high-flying career of an imperial officer. The models for Vera's distant parents, more caught up in their social lives than in the education of their three daughters, are recognizable from Kovalevskaya's childhood memoir. Her depiction of the fear, incomprehension, and disintegration of the Barantsov family following Alexander II's decree emancipating the serfs likely presents a composite picture of the often negative social and economic consequences of that momentous event for landowners and peasants alike. As Vera develops from being a conventional bread-and-butter miss who is first infatuated by the lives of Christian martyrs and then comes to an awareness of more realistic social goals, her maturation closely follows the life of Kovalevskaya's sister, who became a prominent feminist and socialist in France during the Commune of 1870-71. For both the real-life sisters and for Vera, an older male figure awakens a young girl's mind to the world beyond her sheltered childhood, mapping out the more active and self-determined role she can play in her adult life. For Sonya and Anyuta, it was a seminarian; for Vera, Vasiltsev, a professor who is fired from his position at the Saint Petersburg Technological Institute and exiled to his estate. Details that include dress style, reading preferences, and physical comportment coincide in many instances for all three female characters.

It is also plausible that another prototype for Vera's character, and an influence on the lives of both Sofya and Anyuta, can be found in the life and writings of the utopian socialist writer and paragon of self-sacrifice and social engagement, Chernyshevsky. Many scholars have examined the profound effect that his novel, *What Is to Be Done?*, with its sweeping program for radically changing Russian life, had on the generations of young, progressive, and radical Russians who laid the groundwork not only for reform but also for revolution in Russia. Even more to the point, Paperno has noted "the special impact of Chernyshevsky's novel," and of Chernyshevsky's life as well, on the Korvin-Krukovsky sisters (33). In addition to *Nihilist Girl*, at the time of her death Kovalevskaya left behind an unfinished fragment of another novella, *Nihilist*, based on the figure of Chernyshevsky.

While sharing a first name with Vera Pavlovna, the energetic heroine of Chernyshevsky's novel, Vera Barantsova is in no way a clone of that famously independent and intelligent "new woman." Rather, the heroine of *Nihilist Girl* epitomizes a different, but equally important, feature of the Russian revolutionary impulse, one that Richard Stites has characterized as "religious feeling without religious faith" (150). For both Vera and Chernyshevsky, who was the son of a provincial priest and a seminarian, social consciousness is shaped by the stories of saints' lives. Vera reads them as a lonely, alienated provincial girl, dreaming of following in the footsteps of recent Christian martyrs persecuted in China. When Vasiltsev, a well-meaning, older neighbor and another in a long list of nineteenth-century Russia's "superfluous men," opens her eyes to Russia's devastating problems, Vera's passion for martyrdom disappears, replaced by a fervid but unformed desire to find an alternative calling, for it is not the theology but the paradigms of self-sacrifice and loss of identity that move her. The opening and closing chapters of *Nihilist Girl*, set in 1874, tell the tale of the displacement of Vera's religious feeling to the arena of social action.[8]

The course of action that Vera Barantsova finally settles on assumes the features of a classic, Christian feat, now shifted to a revolutionary cause. Grounded in the desire to do unmediated good, unwilling to follow formalized solutions, she would seem to replicate Chernyshevsky's life and novel: both Vera Pavlovna, in her quest for spiritual development, and Chernyshevsky himself, with his secular martyrdom at the hands of the police, his arrest, and subsequent sanctification by the liberal intelligentsia, likely contributed to Kovalevskaya's imagining of her heroine. Despite these close connections between the two works, however, it would be a mistake to identify *Nihilist Girl* as a simulacrum of Chernyshevsky's novel. Unwilling in her writing as in her life to adopt reductionist views of politics, gender, or class, Kovalevskaya does not make an icon of her heroine. While she sympathizes with her, she is well aware of her limitations, as is Vera herself. Vera's confession to the narrator, just before she leaves for Siberia with her new "husband," is key to understanding her temperament and her predicament:

> And to think that I moped about all last winter looking for work [. . .]. But it was here, right at hand, and what work it is! I couldn't have thought up anything better. I can tell you in all honesty: I probably would not have been any good at anything like revolutionary propaganda or conspiracy. For that you need a great mind, eloquence, the ability to affect people, to bring them under your leadership, and I have none of that.

While this statement can be read as the modesty topos encountered in hagiographic literature (or in the psyches of young girls), it also brings to light the difficulty that nihilist women typically had in realizing the personal and social goals they had set for themselves. The combination of restrictive laws and traditions regarding education and employment opportunities for women, the absence of a network of emotional support, and the young women's own upbringing and habits frequently worked against them. Barbara Engel has observed that "few [nihilist women] became as prominent or as political as Anna [Anyuta Korvin-Krukovskaya Jaclard]" (67) or, for that matter, as her sister Sofya. All in all, Kovalevskaya has drawn Vera as a willing but ill-prepared fighter for a good cause. Vera's lot is in many ways better than that of other radical women. By the time she turns twenty, her family has conveniently left the stage, and, as heiress to a modest annual income, she leaves her estate with barely a second thought. Once in Saint Petersburg, she appears at the narrator's doorstep, in search of "a purpose, a goal in life." Clueless as to what to do with her new independence, bored by the study of science and the readings of the major radical political and economic theorists of her day recommended by the narrator, and lacking any useful skills, she finally chooses an avenue for action that will save one man but do little to reform traditional institutions, let alone undo tsarist oppression.

In marrying the political prisoner Pavlenkov, Vera executes an ideological reversal that can be understood only in terms of Christian charity and self-sacrifice. Russian women with radical ideals typically acquired a higher education to pursue communitarian goals: to teach or treat "the people," that is, the recently emancipated peasants, and to change tsarist society, through peaceful and, eventually for some, violent tactics. Vera's scope and goals are much narrower. Vera willingly sacrifices her own autonomy by marrying a political prisoner not of her class, a man she barely knows and certainly does not love, a Jew in an emphatically anti-Semitic society (as the account of the group trial shows), a person whom the narrator finds rather unattractive physically. The image of a wife following her dissident husband into Siberian exile will remind any historically literate Russian reader of Princess Volkonskaya and other wives of the Decembrists, aristocratic participants in an unsuccessful revolt in 1825, but those wives followed their husbands out of love and uxorial devotion. Here, love plays a role in Vera's decision, but it is a displaced emotion. As she marries Pavlenkov in the prison chapel, she becomes distracted and "it seemed to me that it was not Pavlenkov standing beside me, but Vasiltsev, and I could hear his dear voice clearly and distinctly," she tells the narrator.[9]

Thus *Nihilist Girl* lends itself to a dual reading, as a model of a historical type and as a critique of that model. In creating a female character who is an amalgam of traditional and new ideas about women's roles and motivations, Kovalevskaya presents a complex answer to issues of feminism and radical activity, to the relation of the woman question to other areas of social, political, and economic reform. Given the author's experiences in both her personal and public life with the egalitarian promises of progressive social thought, *Nihilist Girl* marks a certain retreat from or, at least, disappointment with those promises. The narrator's (and probably Kovalevskaya's) admiration for her heroine's single-mindedness goes hand in hand with sympathy for the lack of real choices open to the heroine. Haphazardly educated, short on self-confidence, and unimpressed by socialist utopian scenarios, Vera makes choices that reflect the complex self-imposed and external constraints on women's ability to gain authority over their own lives.

Jane Costlow, writing about the lack of positive heroines in women's writing in the 1860s and 1870s, finds a "disinclination to imagine utopian solutions to what were [. . .] intimate and intractable problems" (63). While there is the suggestion of female camaraderie between Vera and other convicts' wives and mothers as they leave for Siberia at the end of *Nihilist Girl*, it is a tenuous glimmer, for little in her previous experience suggests an inclination to work for communitarian solutions or to support other women in various shared housing and work situations. In the months between Vera and the narrator's first acquaintance and Vera's *podvig* ("heroic deed"), the two women are not in close contact. What starts out as a potentially strong close female relationship ends with Vera's departure for Siberia.[10] Despite Vera's first appeal to the narrator to help her discover how to be "of use to the 'cause,'" she undertakes strictly on her own the difficult task of convincing the authorities to allow her to marry Pavlenkov, invoking family connections in high places to achieve her goal. This initiative can be read positively, as a sign of Vera's maturation, but it may also underscore her rejection of the narrator's solutions for social transformation.

Because most of the commentators on Kovalevskaya's novella have been historians or biographers, there has been little consideration of *Nihilist Girl* as a literary text. Certainly, the work is shaped by the conventions of Russian critical realism of the end of the second half of the nineteenth century, not least in its use of a literary type as a crucible for exploring social issues. Vera's coming to consciousness and pursuit of a self-defined if not fully articulated destiny follow the trajectory of the bildungsromans popular at the time. Catriona Kelly has observed that "the escape plot" was "the backbone of the realist tradition as practiced by women writers, after 1881 as before" (135). In fact, authors ranging from Avdotya Panaeva in the 1850s through Anastasiya Verbitskaya at the end of the century use their heroine's alienation and departure from stifling families and provincial lives as a fulcrum for their narratives. The scrupulously detailed, often ironically portrayed interplay of different classes living on one estate in Vera's childhood brings to mind Sergey Aksakov and Lev Tolstoy, understandably with gender and generationally defined variations on those familiar Russian themes. Vera's precocious love for her forty-something neighbor, when she is fifteen, follows a Turgenevesque pattern of encounter between ingenue and older idealistic man, an encounter that is formative, if almost invariably disappointing, for the young woman. The figure of Vera herself, with her taciturn, solitary temperament and her lonely childhood in communion with nature and vicarious experience of life, alludes to Pushkin's Tatyana in *Eugene Onegin* as well as to numerous other sentimental heroines from Russian and European literature.

We know from *A Russian Childhood* and her many letters that Kovalevskaya took her literary ambitions seriously, especially toward the end of her life. Occasional lapses in Vera's character or motivation leave the reader with a feeling of underdevelopment, or incompleteness. Moreover, the switch in narrative voice is not always felicitous, especially when the first-person narrator of the introduction shifts with no explanation into an omniscient third person for the important middle section. Kovalevskaya compensates for these faults, however, in her eye for telling detail, the naturalness of narrative diction, and the able use of irony. In particular, the childhood and courtroom scenes have the vividness of a firsthand observer keenly involved in what she sees, be it the myriad natural, cultural, psychological, or social details that form a young girl's consciousness; the astute descriptions; or the multiple interests of participants in public events.

As a woman who has experienced the complexities of conjoining public and private lives, Kovalevskaya adopts a stance that is both sympathetic to and distanced from her heroine. Two models of feminine behavior are articulated in *Nihilist Girl*: that of Vera, a young woman looking for a socially meaningful way to put to use such traditional feminine qualities as devotion and self-sacrifice, and that of the narrator, a single professional woman who is independent inwardly and self-reliant outwardly. Although the age difference between the two is not great, the narrator seems much more mature than Vera; not only has the narrator had a broader range of experiences but she is better read, better informed, and more observant of her society. Nevertheless, there is no hierarchy of characterization in *Nihilist Girl*. The three main characters—Vera, narrator, and Vasiltsev—each have limitations and redeeming qualities. While the two women are defined in the narrative as opposites who choose radically different paths to serve their country, they are neither hostile nor mutually contradictory. It is plausible that Kovalevskaya, writing for a foreign audience, intended to suggest that both types were what Russia needed, namely, dedicated, self-sacrificing, and passionate martyr-revolutionaries combined with a professional class. Kovalevskaya takes pains to enlighten the reader about the strengths and limitations of both types, a classic literary maneuver. However, by inserting herself into her narrative and calling on her readers' familiarity with her own biography, she draws on the circularity of art and life to name the woman question in her own terms.

Notes

[1] Fyodor Dostoevsky's *A Writer's Diary* (1873–81) is perhaps the most telling example of this type of hybrid genre.

[2] Most of the biographical information on Sofya Kovalevskaya comes from Koblitz.

[3] Kovalevskaya was awarded corresponding membership in the academy, a notch below an appointment as a full member. Corresponding membership was the status normally given to foreigners and recipients of degrees from foreign universities; her receiving it represented a significant achievement, since the academy's rules had to be changed to permit her membership at all.

[4] By coincidence, she fell in love with Maxim Kovalevsky, a distant cousin of her dead husband, who was a sociologist and law professor living in Paris after his dismissal from Moscow University for his radical teachings.

[5] Most of Kovalevskaya's other writings consisted of unpublished poetry; a two-part play, *The Struggle for Happiness (How It Was and How It Might Have Been)*, cowritten with Leffler; fragments of stories; and a number of profiles and sketches that were published in several major Petersburg journals and newspapers. For information on her other publications, see Koblitz, chapter 14; Putintsev's introduction to the 1960 Russian edition of *Nihilist Girl*.

[6] Indeed, Pozefsky notes "the suspicion with which members of the next generation of radicals, the so-called populists, looked upon [the generation of the 1860s]. Many populists regarded the emphasis on scientific research, practiced exclusively by intellectuals, as elitist" (363). See also Gleason, chapter 2, for a succinct discussion of the nuances within the movement.

[7] Readers familiar with Kovalevskaya's characterization of her sister Anna (Anyuta) in *A Russian Childhood* will recognize her presence in *Nihilist Girl* as well.

[8] Another reminder that fact underlies the fiction of Kovalevskaya's novella is that the given name of all three heroines—Vera Barantsova; Vera Goncharova, her real life prototype; and Chernyshevsky's Vera Pavlovna—means "faith" in Russian.

[9] Underscoring the fictive element in Kovalevskaya's tale is the fact that Vera Goncharova's goals were not so narrow as Vera Barantsova's. Koblitz notes that Goncharova was one of the first four women to enroll in the Sorbonne's medical program.

[10] Here again, biography and fiction diverge. In real life, Kovalevskaya found Goncharova very appealing, and Kovalevskaya was the one who actually arranged Goncharova's encounters with I. Ya. Pavlovsky. Moreover, relations between the women of the 1860s and populist women were in fact quite close.

Works Cited

Chernyshevsky, Nikolay. *What Is to Be Done?* Trans. and ed. Michael Katz. Ithaca: Cornell UP, 1989.

Costlow, Jane. "Love, Work, and the Woman Question in Mid-Nineteenth-Century Women's Writing." *Women Writers in Russian Literature.* Ed. Toby W. Clyman and Diana Greene. Westport: Praeger, 1994. 61–75.

Dostoevsky, Fyodor M. *A Writer's Diary.* Evanston: Northwestern UP, 1997.

Engel, Barbara A. *Mothers and Daughters: Women of the Intelligentsia in Nineteenth-Century Russia.* Cambridge: Cambridge UP, 1983.

Gleason, Abbott. *Young Russia: The Genesis of Russian Radicalism in the 1860s.* Chicago: U of Chicago P, 1980.

Kelly, Catriona. *A History of Russian Women's Writing, 1820-1992.* Oxford: Clarendon, 1994.

Koblitz, Ann Hibner. *A Convergence of Lives: Sofia Kovalevskaia: Scientist, Writer, Revolutionary.* Trenton: Rutgers UP, 1993.

Kovalevskaia, Sof'ia V. *A Russian Childhood.* Trans. and ed. Beatrice Stillman. New York: Springer, 1978.

———. *Vospominaniia i pis'ma* [*Reminiscences and Correspondence*]. 2nd ed. Moscow: Akademiia nauk, 1961.

McReynolds, Louise, and Cathy Popkin. "The Objective Eye and the Common Good." *Constructing Russian Culture in the Age of Revolution, 1881–1940.* Ed. Catriona Kelly and David Shepherd. Oxford: Oxford UP, 1998. 57–105.

Paperno, Irina. *Chernyshevsky and the Age of Realism: A Study in the Semiotics of Behavior.* Stanford: Stanford UP, 1988.

Pozefsky, Peter. "Love, Science, and Politics in the Fiction of *Shestidesiatnitsy* N. P. Suslova and S. V. Kovalevskaya." *Russian Review* 58 (1999): 361–79.

Putintsev, Vladimir A. "Literaturnoe nasledie Sof'i Kovalevskoi" [Sof'ia Kovalevskaia's Literary Legacy]. *Vospominaniia detstva [and] Nigilistka.* Moscow: Khudozhestvennaia literatura, 1960. 3–15.

Stites, Richard. *The Women's Liberation Movement in Russia: Feminism, Nihilism, and Bolshevism, 1860–1930.* Princeton: Princeton UP, 1978.

Turgenev, Ivan. *Fathers and Sons.* Trans. George Reavy. New York: Signet, 1989.

SHORT BIBLIOGRAPHY OF WORKS BY AND ABOUT
Sofya Kovalevskaya

Koblitz, Ann Hibner. "Career and Home Life in the 1880s: The Choices of Mathematician Sofia Kovalevskaia." *Uneasy Careers and Intimate Lives: Women in Science 1789–1979*. Ed. Pnina G. Abir-Am. New Brunswick: Rutgers UP, 1987.

Kochina, Pelageya. *Love and Mathematics: Sof'ia Kovalevskaia.* Moscow: Mir, 1985.

Koltonovskaia, Elena A. *Zhenskie siluety: Pisatel'nitsy i artistki.* [Feminine Silhouettes: Artists and Writers]. Saint Petersburg: Prosvieshchenie, 1912.

Kotliarevskii, N. A. "Nigilistka." *Strana* 3-16 Sept. 1906: 2.

Kovalevskaia, Sof'ia. *Izbrannye proizvedeniia* [Selected Works]. Moscow: Sovetskaia Rossia, 1982.

———. *Literaturnye sochineniia* [Literary Works]. Saint Petersburg: Stasiulevicha, 1893.

———. *Nigilistka.* Geneva: Vol'naia russkaia, 1892. 2nd ed. 1899.

———. *Nigilistka.* Moscow: Kokhmanskogo, 1906. Rpt. in *Svidanie.* Ed. Viktoriia V. Uchenova. Moscow: Sovremennik, 1987.

———. *Nigilistka.* Khar'kov: Proletarii, 1928.

———. *Vera Barantsova.* Trans. Sergius Stepniak and William Westall. London: Ward, 1895.

———. *Vera Vorontzoff.* Trans. Anna von Rydingsvard. Boston: Lamson, 1895.

———. *Vospominaniia detstva* [Memoirs of Childhood] [*and*]

Nigilistka. Moscow: Khudozhestvennaia literatura, 1960.

————.*Vospominaniia i avtobiograficheskie ocherki* [Memoirs and Autobiographical Sketches]. Moscow: Akademii nauk, 1945.

————. *Vospominaniia, povesti* [Memoirs, Novellas]. Ed. Pelageia Ia. Polubarinova-Kochina. Moscow: Akademii nauk, 1974. Moscow: "Pravda," 1986.

————."Vstrechi s V. S. Goncharovoi" [Meetings with V. S. Goncharova]. *Vospominaniia i pis'ma* [Memoirs and Correspondence]. Ed. Solomon Ia. Shtraikh. Moscow: Akademii nauk, 1951. 2nd ed. 1961. 183–202.

Ledkovsky, Marina, et al., eds. *Dictionary of Russian Women Writers*. Westport: Greenwood, 1994.

Marcus, Jane. "The Private Selves of Public Women." *The Private Self: Theory and Practice of Women's Autobiographical Writings*. Ed. Sheri Benstock. Chapel Hill: U of North Carolina P, 1988. 126–34.

Naginski, Isabelle. "A Nigilistka and a Communard: Two Voices of the Nineteenth-Century Intelligentka." *Woman as Mediatrix: Essays on Nineteenth-Century European Women Writers*. Ed. Avriel H. Goldberger. New York: Hofstra UP, 1987. 145–58.

Polubarinova-Kochina, Pelageia Ia., ed. *Pamiati S. V. Kovalevskoi: Sbornik statei* [In Memory of S. V. Kovalevskaia: A Collection of Articles]. Moscow: Akademii nauk, 1951.

————. *Zhizn' i deiatel'nost' S. V. Kovalevskoi* [The Life and Career of S. V. Kovalevskaia]. Moscow: Akademii nauk, 1950.

Stillman, Beatrice. "Sofya Kovalevskaya: Growing Up in the Sixties." *Russian Literature Triquarterly* 9 (1974): 276–302.

Zirin, Mary. "Anna Vasil'evna Korvin-Krukovskaia." Ledkovsky et al. 322–24.

————. "Sofia Vasil'evna Kovalevskaia." Ledkovsky et al. 328–29.

Suggestions for Further Reading

These passages and books (full bibliographic information given if the work is not in the preceding Works Cited) are recommended: Chernyshevsky 1–36; Costlow; Engel, 62–66, 83–84, 201; Gleason; Barbara Heldt, *Terrible Perfection: Women and Russian Literature* (Bloomington: Indiana UP, 1987) 66; Kelly 50–63, 121–38; Ann H. Koblitz, *Science, Women, and Revolution in Russia* (Amsterdam: Harwood Academic, 2000); Margaret Maxwell, *Narodniki Women* (New York: Pergamon, 1990) 48; McReynolds and Popkin; Paperno 17–19, 33–36, 274–75; Nataliia L. Pushkareva, *Women in Russian History from the Tenth to the Twentieth Century*, ed. and trans. Eve Levin (Armonk: Sharpe, 1997) 201–15; Stites; Mary Zirin, "Women's Prose Fiction in the Age of Realism," *Women Writers in Russian Literature*, ed. Toby W. Clyman and Diana Greene (Westport: Praeger, 1994) 77–94.

ABOUT THE TEXT AND TRANSLATION

The present volume is the first translation into English of the 1892 Geneva edition of Kovalevskaya's *Nihilist Girl*. It is a translation of the text in her *Vospominaniia detstva [and] Nigilistka* (1960), the only modern edition with *nigilistka* in its title. A later edition, also based on the Geneva edition, appeared in 1974 and was reprinted in 1987, in *Svidanie*, a collection of works by nineteenth-century Russian women writers.

In his notes to the 1960 edition, V. A. Putintsev suggests that Kovalevskaya, knowing that her novella would not pass censorship in Imperial Russia, first wrote a version of *Nihilist Girl* in Swedish in 1883-84 with the intent of publishing it, or its translation, somewhere in Europe. In 1889–90, she rewrote that earlier version, this time in Russian. At the time of her death, two different drafts, substantially revised and expanded from the original Swedish, remained. Her friends Anna Carlotta Leffler and Ellen Key, together with her fiancé, Maksim Kovalevsky, edited the two texts into a final version and published the novella in Russian in Geneva in 1892, with subsequent editions in 1895 and 1899.

Because of its caustic portrayal of the tsarist courts' treatment of political prisoners—a good part of the action takes place in 1874, during a period of crackdowns on political activists in Russia—the imperial censorship forbade including the novella in a posthumous collection of Kovalevskaya's literary works that appeared in Moscow in 1893. Copies of Swedish, German, French, Polish, Czech, and English translations were regularly smuggled into Russia, but *Nihilist Girl* did not legally appear in its author's native land until 1906, during a period of relative liberalization following the "revolution" of 1905. A petition forwarded to the censors in 1915 for another edition was rejected, and the novella remained out of print until 1928, when the first Soviet edition appeared, with the misleading title *Proletarii*.

The non-Russian versions of Kovalevskaya's novella (sometimes with the alternative title of its eponymous heroine, *Vera Barantsova* or *Vera Vorontsova*) vary widely in their textual faithfulness and completeness. Of two versions published in English, both in 1895, neither follows the first 1892 Russian-language edition published in Geneva. Each was heavily abridged, and the American version, *Vera Vorontsoff*, was almost certainly translated from the early Swedish version and deviates substantially from the first Russian edition.

Douglas Hofstadter, in his witty anagram of the word translation (*translation = lost in an art*; 136), captures the myriad joys and pitfalls of my attempt to transform *Nigilistka* into *Nihilist Girl*. As with any text, this version of *Nihilist Girl* presents a negotiation between accuracy and stylistic considerations. Russian is much freer when it comes to the use of tense, so that deciding on a tense and staying with it has been a major problem. Kovalevskaya's narrator adopts a perky, often colloquial, at times sardonic tone in speaking about her heroine. Avoiding the present perfect tense—the use of which is perfectly natural in Russian but deadly in English—has been the greatest challenge in conveying that tone. It has also seemed essential to me to render as closely as possible the author's semantics, which is that of a cultured, well-read European of the nineteenth century who, when she errs, does so in the direction of literariness rather than sensationalism.

Like many literary works, *Nihilist Girl* has its share of inconsistencies. Some of these are doubtless attributable to the collective posthumous editorial effort, but others suggest that Kovalevskaya's literary skills were still developing. The quality of the writing is sometimes uneven. Kovalevskaya's descriptions of the physical and psychic spaces of her heroine's childhood, and her gift for satire and sly observation, reveal an author with a keen eye and the ability to re-create that vision verbally. At other times, as the narrator fast-forwards through critical, formative times in her heroine's life, compresses her development, or abruptly shifts a setting or mood, one wishes that the author had had a sharper editorial eye and more time. Such qualities, however, are beyond a translator's powers of transformation.

Note

For the sake of pronunciation and common sense, I use a nonspecialist's transliteration of Cyrillic names and titles in the introduction, text, and footnotes to *Nihilist Girl*. In all references in the bibliography, however, I have used the Library of Congress transliteration system. Thus the author's name is rendered as Sofya Kovalevskaya in the text, but Sof'ia Kovalevskaia in the bibliographical references to Russian sources.

Work Cited

Hofstadter, Douglas R. *Le Ton Beau de Marot: In Praise of the Music of Language.* New York: Basic, 1997.

SOFYA KOVALEVSKAYA

Nihilist Girl

I

I was twenty-two years old when I moved to Petersburg. Three months earlier I had graduated from a university abroad and returned to Russia, doctoral degree in hand. After five years of isolated, cloistered existence in a small university town, life in Petersburg immediately enveloped and, as it were, intoxicated me. Putting aside for a while the consideration of analytic functions, space, and the four dimensions, which had so recently obsessed me, I threw myself into new interests. I made acquaintances left and right. I tried to penetrate the most varied circles. With greedy curiosity, I turned my attention to all the essentially empty but initially so engaging manifestations of that complex hubbub that we call life in Petersburg.

It was a time when everything interested and pleased me. Theaters, benefit galas, and literary circles with their endless discussions of every kind of abstract topic ultimately leading nowhere—every bit of it entertained me. The usual habitués of these circles had long since grown bored with these debates, but for me they retained all the charm of novelty. I surrendered to them with all the passion of a naturally talkative Russian who had spent five years among German ways in the sole company of two or three specialists, each involved in his own narrow, all-absorbing work, with no thought of wasting valuable time on idle chatter.

The pleasure that I took in being with other people spread to those around me. My own enthusiasm introduced a novel animation and life into the circle in which I moved. My reputation as a learned woman surrounded me with a certain aura: my acquaintances expected something extraordinary from me. Already, two or three journals had trumpeted my existence. While the role of "celebrated woman"—quite new to me—was somewhat embarrassing, it also amused me as I took these first steps. In short, I was in a most benevolent frame of mind; experiencing my honeymoon of fame, so to speak, and readily would have exclaimed during this period of my life: "All is for the best in the best of all possible worlds."

On this particular day, I was in a particularly benevolent frame of mind. I had spent the previous evening in the offices of a newly inaugurated journal, to which I had been asked to contribute. This new undertaking aroused the lively enthusiasm of all its contributors, and our Saturday editorial meetings were notable for being exceptionally animated. I had returned home after two in the morning, got up late, lingered over my morning tea, and glanced through several newspapers with interest. I saw an advertisement for a carved bookcase on sale secondhand and went to take a look at it. On the way, on the horse-drawn tram, I met a lady I knew who was a fellow member of the committee on the newly opened higher women's courses.[1] I discussed

---

[1] The Petersburg Higher Courses of Education for Women, popularly known as the Bestuzhev courses, were the best known and most enduring of the women's "universities" created in the 1870s. Kovalevskaya

4

business with her, paid visits to two or three other acquaintances, and returned home around four. Sitting in a comfortable armchair in front of a blazing fire, I scrutinized my handsome study with pleasure. After five years of hardship in various furnished rooms let by German landladies, I was quite sensitive to the novel pleasure of having my own cozy corner. The doorbell rang.

"Who can that be?" I wondered, mentally scrolling through the names of my various acquaintances. I took a quick anxious glance in the mirror to be sure that I was presentable.

A tall young woman wearing a simple cloth coat walked into the room. Because of my nearsightedness, I couldn't immediately decide whether I knew her or not, especially since a black scarf concealed most of her face. Only a small, straight nose, slightly reddened from the cold, remained exposed. I got up to greet my guest amiably, although with a certain perplexity in my gaze.

"Excuse me for disturbing you, since we're not personally acquainted," she said. "I'm Vera Barantsova. It's unlikely that you'll remember my name, though our parents owned neighboring estates. I've recently read about you in the newspapers. I know that you've spent a long time studying abroad, and that everyone's talking about you.

---

served on the executive committee, but she plays with the dates here, since the courses did not open their doors until 1878 and Kovalevskaya had returned to Petersburg in 1874.

5

They say you're a good person, a serious person, so it occurred to me that you could give me some advice."

The new arrival said all of this hurriedly, and breathlessly in an extremely pleasant, deep voice. I was both puzzled and flattered by this evidence of my fame. This was the first time a stranger had turned to me for advice.

"Why, I'm very pleased. Do sit down. And take off your coat," I mumbled cordially. I, too, was exceedingly embarrassed.

Vera took off the black scarf. I was struck by her beauty.

"I'm all alone in the world and depend on no one. My personal life is over. I don't expect or want anything for myself. My passionate, my fervent wish is to be of use to 'the cause.' Tell me, teach me what to do," she said all of a sudden, without preface, immediately broaching the purpose of her visit.

From anyone else, this strange, unexpected beginning might have come as an unpleasant surprise, might have seemed a contrived attempt to make an impression on me. But Vera spoke so simply, and with such a sincere, anxious, and beseeching note in her voice, that I wasn't in the least taken aback.

This tall, graceful young woman, with her pale, smooth face and her thoughtful dark-blue eyes, suddenly seemed uncommonly familiar and attractive to me. I was afraid only that I wouldn't justify her trust, that I couldn't supply a proper response to her request, that I couldn't give her useful advice. My personal life over the last three or four months suddenly seemed empty and trivial. All my absorbing interests suddenly lost their sense and significance. A sudden pang of conscience pierced my heart. What could I say to her? How could I help her?

Not knowing where to begin, I invited Vera to take a seat and ordered tea. In Russia, heart-to-heart talks can't take place without a samovar. What struck me about Vera from the first hour of our acquaintance was her complete indifference to external matters. She was like those visionaries so struck by an object only they can see that they are oblivious to other impressions. I asked whether she'd been in Petersburg for long, whether she was comfortably settled in a hotel. Vera answered all these banal questions absentmindedly, and with a trace of dissatisfaction. Life's trivia evidently made no claims on her attention. Although this was her first stay in Petersburg, life in the capital neither surprised nor interested her. She was completely engrossed in a single thought—to find a purpose, a goal in life. I felt a strong attraction to this young woman, who so little resembled anyone I'd ever known. This was why I wanted to earn her trust, to learn her most secret thoughts. I answered that I couldn't give her advice until I knew her better. I asked her to visit me as often as she could and to tell me all about her past. Vera could only think about how best to express herself, answering all my questions with abrupt candor. Within a few weeks I had penetrated her heart and begun to read it as clearly as it is possible for one woman to read another's.

II

The family of the counts Barantsov was a distinguished and noble one, although it could not be said to have an ancient lineage. True, its official genealogy had been traced back almost to Ryurik,[2] but the total reliability of this document is in some doubt. It has been fully ascertained only that one Ivashka Barantsov was a private in Her Majesty Empress Catherine II's regiment,[3] that he had a milk-and-honey complexion, was one *sazhen* tall,[4] and managed to serve the Little Mother Empress so well that for his faithful service he was immediately promoted to corporal and granted an estate of five hundred peasants and one thousand rubles—in those days, peasants were cheap and money was dear. From that time on, the Barantsovs began to flourish. Alexander I, at whose court the Countess Barantsova played a visible role for a time, bestowed on the family the title of count. However, chronicles of this sort enumerate not only successes in the last hundred years: the family also suffered some setbacks.

---

[2] The Danish Prince Ryurik and his brothers are reputed to be the founding princes of Kievan Russia, in the ninth century.

[3] Empress Catherine II (the Great), born the German princess Sophia Frederika Augusta, reigned from 1762 to 1796. Her son, Paul I, ruled briefly, from 1796 to 1801. Upon his death, Russia was ruled from 1801 to 1825 by Paul's oldest son, Alexander I. From 1825 to 1855, Alexander's brother, Nicholas I, was on the throne. Most of *Nihilist Girl* takes place during the reign of his son, Alexander II, who was crowned emperor in 1855 and assassinated in 1881.

[4] A *sazhen* is 2.13 meters.

All the Barantsovs were distinguished by their ardor and their unbridled desires, and more than once this trait brought them to grief. They gambled away more than one rich estate, more than one lucrative provincial post over the years in card games, or spent it on horses and beautiful women. A temporary cloud would settle over the fate of the Barantsov family then, but, through the grace of God, it was soon dissipated by the sun of imperial grace. One of the Barantsovs always contrived to perform some service for the tsar and the fatherland just in the nick of time, and new splendid estates appeared to replace the lost ones so that, all in all, the family continued to grow and prosper. Moreover, while estates were quickly lost and quickly gained in this clan, there was one valuable legacy that invariably passed from generation to generation, from father to son and from mother to daughter—their unusual, so to speak, familial beauty. All the Barantsovs were handsome. It's not that they produced no monstrous or ugly children, but rather that even plain ones were not to be found among them. As if they were experiencing a natural attraction toward beauty or instinctively foreshadowing Darwin, all the count Barantsovs married beautiful women and all their daughters found handsome husbands, so that now the family type had established itself so solidly and was so well-known in the Russian aristocracy that if someone were to say to you, he or she is the picture of a Barantsov, and if a distinct image didn't come to mind immediately—

tall, stately stature; a smooth, white, oblong face with a slight, transparent blush; a low, broad forehead with a delicate pattern of bluish veins at the temples; raven-black hair; and dark-blue eyes with black eyelashes—then you were not a member of the aristocracy and understood nothing about the ways of Russia's *upper ten thousands*.[5]

This Barantsov type is so durable and vital that in the good old days of serfdom it was even observed to be capable of passing to peasants and to the household staff on the counts' estates. An amazing business! All the lords and masters or young gentlemen had to do was spend time on their estates, and invariably, in some peasant cottage or another—always, moreover, in those where the women were young and attractive—a child would be born who was, well, the very image of a little Barantsov, with the same delicate, noble facial features as those of the children in the manor house.

Count Mikhail Ivanovich Barantsov was a worthy scion of the clan. A handsome man, he was lucky to have been born at the beginning of Nicholas I's reign, just at the moment that the Petersburg guard was reaching its peak. After serving several years in the cuirassier regiment and conquering many feminine hearts—thereby honestly earning among his comrades the flattering nickname "tormentor of husbands"—the count, still a young man, fell head

---

[5] In English in the original.

over heels in love with Mariya Dmitrievna Kudryavtseva, a distant relative who also carried the stamp of the Barantsov line on a face so beautiful that it looked as if it had been chiseled by a great sculptor. Finding his feelings reciprocated, he married and continued to serve in the guard. He might have attained high rank, but at the beginning of Alexander II's reign, there was a minor incident whose cause could also be traced to that tempestuous Barantsov blood and fateful Barantsov beauty. Jealous of another officer's attentions to his lovely wife, the young count challenged him to a duel and shot him dead. The affair was instantly swept under the rug, but it was awkward for the young count to remain in his regiment: he was forced to submit his resignation and retire to the estate he had just inherited from his father, who had died just in time.

That was in 1857. Vague rumors were already afoot in Petersburg about the imminent emancipation of the serfs, but these had not yet reached Borki, as the Barantsov estate was called, and the time-honored practices still prevailed. No one knew the exact scope of Count Mikhail Ivanovich's wealth, least of all the count himself. The estate was quite extensive, though far from what it had once been. His deceased papa, God rest his soul, had also liked to live for pleasure, so that a large portion of the forest had been chopped down and more than a few dessiatines[6] of

---

[6] One dessiatine (*desiatina*) is 2.7 acres.

meadowland sold during his lifetime. As one might imagine, after almost fifteen years of service in the cuirassiers, Mikhail Ivanovich didn't leave Petersburg debt-free. He began his management of the estate by selling off another sizable piece of land to pay off old sins, mortgaging the rest. Nonetheless, at least for the time being, everything seemed to be in good order, and no one troubled the count with details. The village elder was a fine fellow, capable of arranging matters without too much fussing or discussing. When the master needed money, it was always readily available.

In spite of their three growing daughters, at the time of their move to the countryside, Count Mikhail Ivanovich and Countess Mariya Dmitrievna remained and continued to think of themselves as very young people. They knew no worries or responsibilities, and no one denied them the right to live their lives purely for pleasure.

Once in the country, they continued with their free and merry ways. When the deceased master had still been alive, the household had been run in a generous, even lordly manner: thirty riding horses in the stable, an English garden, hothouses and conservatories, and a mass of useless, lazy domestic servants. The sole change that the new masters brought to the conceits of the old was the addition of many refined and varied frills imported from the capital, frills undreamt of in the countryside before their arrival. They upholstered all the furniture in the formal rooms in silk. Before, the floors and windows had been bare, but now rugs were laid and drapes hung everywhere. Before, the footmen had worn greasy frock coats cast off by their masters, but now livery was tailored just for them. The kitchen was turned over to a chef who had trained at the English Club,[7] while in the maid's quarters, a stylish lady's maid from among the freed serfs was now added to the throng of homespun girls who sewed, embroidered, and made lace from morning to night.

The example of the young masters had a salutary effect on the neighbors as well. It was not without cause that the governor, in his remarks at a dinner given in honor of the new arrivals, noted the new vitality they had brought to the province. Indeed, with their arrival, an era of holidays, feasts, and amusements began. People didn't want to be outdone by their guests from the capital. The landowners and their wives shook off their country laziness, and earlier artless amusements, leaden name-day dinners, card games, and dances were now replaced by more refined and what might be called intellectual pleasures. In the first year after the Barantsovs' move to their estate, the provincial capital was the site of an amateur dramatic performance, a concert with living tableaux, and a masked charity ball by subscription.

Both Mikhail Ivanovich and Mariya Dmitrievna were delighted by the impression that they made in the province,

---

[7] A renowned private club with a famous restaurant in Moscow. It is mentioned in chapter 7 of Pushkin's *Eugene Onegin*, as well as in scenes in Tolstoy's *War and Peace* that take place in Moscow.

and both were quite taken by the importance of what we might call their civilizing mission. At one formal dinner, the count even made a speech about the merits of the English *gentry* and the advisability of transforming Russian landowners into English *landlords*.[8]

The countess also labored at length to ennoble provincial ways, and therefore felt obliged to import expensive dresses from Petersburg. The Barantsov house was always open to guests. Dinner was served late, as in the city, and all the servants changed livery before dinner, as was the custom in England. English vodka, rather than the purified Russian kind, was served with the hors d'oeuvres.

From the outside, the Barantsov house, a ponderous, old-fashioned structure with stone walls about two arshins thick,[9] reminded one of an enormous square box onto which, God knows why, bizarre lanterns and minuscule balconies had been pasted. In general, it was in that distinct style, apparently not noted in architectural textbooks, that might best be called "serf style." There was too much of everything, materials had been carelessly used, and everything was rough and awkward. In all its details, you could see that the house had been built at a time when labor was free and everyone made do with the resources at hand. Serfs had fired the bricks on-site and made the parquet floors of

---

[8] Both words are in English in the original.
[9] An old Russian measure of length, an arshin is about 28 inches.

wood from the estate's forests. Even the architect who had drawn up the plan was a serf.[10] The interior layout of the rooms in the Barantsov house was also indistinguishable from the majority of manor houses of the time: the masters lived upstairs, the nursery was downstairs, and the kitchen and servants' quarters were in the cellar.

The countess came down to the cellar only on Easter, when she exchanged the ritual kisses with the household staff. True, when she had the time on free days—that is, when there were no guests or she wasn't planning to go calling—she did look into the children's rooms, but this didn't happen very often.

The three young Barantsov girls grew up in the nursery of the house under the care of two governesses. One of them, Mlle Julie, was a tall, very lively, and talkative brunette of indeterminate age, while the other, Mme Knight, was a venerable widow with a stern, stony face framed by large gray curls. In addition to the two governesses, a sizable number of other servants also attended to the children: an old nanny, Anisya the chambermaid, and a young errand girl.

In short, everything was as it should be in a respectable manor house. All three young ladies were tall for their age;

---

[10] Beginning in the second half of the eighteenth century, many members of the gentry commissioned their serfs, who were largely self-trained, to design and build manor houses and other structures on the estates.

all three had wonderful thick hair, which was braided into a single braid each morning and loosened around their shoulders at dinnertime; and all three held the promise of becoming in time beautiful young women.

Lena and Liza, the two older girls, were poised, as one might say, on the threshold of the children's room, and soon it would be time for them to flit into the drawing room. Lena was fourteen and Liza thirteen. Both already listened with intense curiosity to every sound that filtered down to them from upstairs, and both complained bitterly that they were still forced to wear short dresses.

The third daughter, Vera, was still very young, only about eight. She had a round rosy face and the strange, contemplative look that is almost always seen in the eyes of children who live their own child's life. For now, she had nothing to complain about. Like all children whose life had gone smoothly, she had well-developed conservative instincts: without realizing it, she was attached to everything around her with the devotion of a well-tended house pet, and it hadn't yet entered her mind to doubt the merits of anyone close to her. Her mama was the best of mamas, her nursery the best of rooms.

Indeed, everything in the Barantsov home went splendidly. Every cricket knew its corner, as we say: all lived in peace and harmony, as is always the case in a society built on solid foundations, one in which no single member is left to beat his head against the wall searching for some separate emotional outlet.

As for love, it was given considerable thought and was the topic of whispers and hopes both downstairs and upstairs in the Barantsov house. Indeed, what else but love's joys and sorrows could, as it were, intersect that straight road, smooth as canvas, that stretched before the three young ladies Barantsov? In all other respects, their lives were predetermined and arranged for them. Mama and Papa had already decided that Mitino would be Lena's dowry, Stepino would go to Liza, and Borki itself would go to the youngest, Vera.[11]

The count and countess also knew that in good time, say in three or four years, a hussar or dragoon would appear without fail to take Lena away. Then, a short while later, another hussar would appear to whisk Liza away. And then Vera's turn would come. Their children would live not in Borki but in another house, and some other maid than Anisya would serve them, but beyond these minor changes, each of the girls would repeat her mama's destiny, just as mama had followed in grandmother's footsteps. All this was very simple and certain, and it went without saying: it was utterly self-evident, just as they knew that there would be dinner tomorrow and the day after.

However, all these certain, unquestionable calculations were suddenly intersected by an unexpected event. Actually,

---

[11] It was common to give different parts of estates different names. Often, as here, these were based on familiar forms of given names. Hence, *Mitino* is derived from *Mitya*, the diminutive for *Dmitry*, and *Stepino* is derived from *Stepan*, the Russian form of *Stephen*.

if the truth be told, this event was not exactly unexpected, since people had been talking about it for twenty years, and all of Russia was preparing for it. Nonetheless, like all momentous events, when it finally happened, it seemed to everyone that it came unexpectedly, catching everyone unawares.

Vera had her first inkling of this imminent event under the following circumstances. Toward the end of 1860, the Barantsovs held a family dinner at which, in addition to the usual aunties, grannies,[12] and close neighbors, a rare and honored guest—an uncle from Petersburg who was an important official in some ministry or other—was in attendance. He had just arrived that morning, and so naturally, he dominated the conversation at dinner, relating various bits of news from the highest official circles, news that you could not, of course, have learned about from the newspapers. Nonetheless, the countess interrupted him several times during dinner, just as his story was becoming most animated.

"*Stépan! Prenez garde,*"[13] she said, mysteriously nodding her head at the footmen carrying around plates, even though no change was discernible in their normal, quite apathetic expressions.

---

[12] Provincial families were usually extended affairs, with various unmarried or widowed relatives of all ages taken under the fold of the more prosperous relatives.

[13] In French: "Stepan! Be careful!" As readers of *War and Peace* will remember, educated Russians often spoke French in polite company. They did so as late as the Russian Revolution.

Everyone moved to the drawing room after dessert. The count himself checked to see that all the doors to the adjacent rooms had been closed.

"*Vous pouvez parler, Stépan!*"[14] he said solemnly.

Vera had already managed to make friends with this new uncle and was sitting on his lap. No one paid attention to her, no doubt thinking that she was too young to understand.

"*C'est fait! L'empereur a souscrit le projet qui lui a été présénté par la commission,*"[15] the fellow solemnly pronounced.

Vera's mama, who had been pouring coffee at that moment, dropped her hands helplessly; the spoon rang against the saucer, and a few drops spilled onto the expensive tablecloth.

"*Mon Dieu! Mon Dieu!*" she said, falling into her armchair and covering her face with her hands.

The others sat as if struck dumb by the fellow's words.

"Is it really possible that it's been decided?" asked Papa in a quiet, forcibly calm voice.

"Absolutely! There's no turning back! The decree will be sent out to all the parish churches at the beginning of February, so that it can be announced to the people on February nineteenth," the uncle answered, stirring his coffee.

---

[14] In French: "You may speak, Stepan!"
[15] In French: "It's done! The emperor has signed the plan presented to him by the commission."

"That means that all we can do now is throw ourselves on God's mercy," sighed Vera's father. This comment was followed by several moments of leaden collective silence.

Suddenly, the voice of old Semyon Ivanovich, Papa's uncle, rang out. "Gentlemen, what is going on? In my opinion, this is out-and-out theft." White hair flying around his flushed, angry face, he jumped up in agitation from his seat and banged the table with his fist.

"For God's sake, Uncle, please don't shout. *Les domestiques peuvent entendre*,"[16] Vera's mama pleaded with him fearfully.

"Well then, explain to me, please, what is going to happen? Does this mean that they will stop obeying us?" elderly Aunt Arina Ivanovna intervened, looking hurt and lost.

"Don't bother us with trifles, sister," Vera's father impatiently pushed her aside with his arm. "Let's ask Stepan about everything so that we have it straight."

The men crowded around Stepan Mikhailovich, who heatedly began to explain something or other. The ladies continued to despair. *"Comment est-ce que l'empereur, qui a l'air si bon, peut nous faire tant de peine?"*[17] one of them wondered.

A servant entered to remove the coffee, and everyone was silent for a moment.

---

[16] In French: "The servants might hear."
[17] In French: "How could the emperor, who seems so kind, bring such grief upon us?"

"Miss, you stayed in the drawing room after dinner today. Did you hear what the masters were discussing?" Anisya asked late that night as she was putting her young lady to bed.

Vera had understood from what was said in the drawing room that a misfortune was threatening the entire family. It hadn't occurred to anyone to tell her to remain silent, but the caste instinct was so strong in this purebred little animal that she answered, with dignity, "I didn't hear anything, Anisya."

Although everyone now knew that the tsar had not only signed the decree but also sent it out to all the parishes, until the last minute of the last day the masters were still afraid that a servant might hear the news. As for the servants, they gave no indication of knowing anything. All their conversations in the foyer and the pantry were silenced just as abruptly, when one of the masters appeared, as were the conversations in the drawing room with the arrival of a servant.

February nineteenth, that terrible date so long anticipated and so fraught with consequences, finally arrived. The entire Barantsov family was going to church, where the priest was to read the decree after mass. By nine that morning, each and every member of the household was dressed and ready. It was a day of feverish, yet solemn, preparations, as if they were going to a funeral. Everyone was afraid to say an unnecessary word. Even the children instinctively felt the importance, the solemnity of the occasion. They were quiet and meek, not daring to ask any questions.

Neat as a pin, two carriages stood at the main entrance to the house: the horses were in their finest harnesses, the coachmen in new caftans. Papa too was dressed in full regalia, in his officer's uniform and medals. Mama wore an expensive velvet mantilla, and the girls were dressed up like dolls.

The count and countess sat in the front of the first carriage, while the three young girls took their seats in the rear. The governesses, the housekeeper, and the estate manager took their places in the second carriage. The remaining servants proceeded to the church on foot. Other than a few young children and crazy Matvey, no one remained at home.

The road to the church was three versts long. During the trip, Mama often raised a perfumed hanky to her face. Papa kept a stern silence.

The entire square in front of the church porch was dark with people. Between two and three thousand peasant men and women from the surrounding villages had gathered. From a distance it looked like one endless mass of gray homespun jackets in the midst of which a bright-red woman's scarf flashed here and there.

"*Ce spectacle me fait mal! Je pense involontairement à '89,*"[18] the countess mumbled hysterically.

---

[18] In French: "This spectacle makes me sick. I can't help but think about [17]89." For the aristocratic countess, talk of the emancipation here brings up the frightening specter of the French Revolution.

"De grâce, taisez vous, ma chère,"[19] the count answered in
an agitated whisper.

Today, as on all holidays, the church's caretaker perched
on the church steeple awaiting the arrival of the masters'
carriage, and as soon as it appeared at the turn of the road,
church bells began to peal.

The church was so packed that there seemed no place for
an apple to fall, yet, as required by an old, deeply rooted tradition, the entire unbroken mass of people respectfully
stepped aside for the masters, allowing them to pass to their
usual spot in front, at the right side of the choir.

"Let us pray to God," intoned the priest, appearing from
behind the altar in full ecclesiastical vestments.

"And to Thy spirit," the choir responded.

On that day, the entire dense, dark-gray mass prayed as
one, intently and ecstatically. The peasants kept making the
sign of the cross and bowing to the ground. Their sallow,
stern faces, deeply furrowed with wrinkles, were distorted
by the intensity of their prayers and expectations.

> Church of lamentation, church of sorrow,
> Wretched church of my land,
> Neither Rome's Saint Peter nor its Colosseum
> Has heard sighs any heavier.[20]

However, today not sighs or moans were heard in the

---

[19] In French: "For God's sake, be quiet, my dear."
[20] This quotation from N. A. Nekrasov's 1857 poem "Tishina"
(Quietude) is inexact.

church. Here, on this day and not only in this church but in the many hundreds of thousands of churches throughout the Russian land, similar fervent prayers, overflowing with boundless faith and passionate hopes, were being recited in unison by one hundred million people, possibly as they had not been recited since the beginning of time.

"Lord, our master! Will Thou have mercy on us? Our sorrow is great and abiding. Will our lives be better henceforth?"

Would the royal decree tell them anything? Until today, even the masters had known its content only from rumors. No one knew anything about it for certain, since copies of the decree had been sent out to the clergy, sealed with an official stamp that would be broken only at the end of the mass.

In spite of the open doors and windows, the exceptionally large crowd of common people and the many lighted candles made the small, cramped church insufferably stifling. The stench of sweaty clothes and dirty boots mingled with the smell of burning candles and fragrant incense. The smoke from the censers rose to the ceiling in blue clouds. Short of air, chests rose heavily and painfully, and the physical discomfort caused by the pained breathing, together with the tension brought on by waiting, gave way to an unbearable sense of distress and inexplicable fear.

"Soon, will it be soon?" the countess whispered hysterically, squeezing her husband's hand convulsively.

The priest brought out the cross. A good half hour passed before everyone had managed to come up to kiss it, but that too finally came to an end. The priest was hidden behind the altar for a moment and then reappeared on the altar steps, holding a roll of embossed paper with a large, official seal hanging from it.

A deep, protracted sigh resounded through the church, as if the whole congregation had breathed as one, with a single chest. Just at that moment there was an unexpected confusion. The huge majority of people who had not been able to make their way into the church and had quietly stayed behind on the porch during the mass now ran out of patience. When the crowd began pushing in concert through the wide-open church doors, something unimaginable happened: people standing in front fell in a heap onto the altar steps. Shouts, curses, groans, and children's squeals rang out.

"*Mon Dieu! Mon Dieu! Prenez pitié de nous!*"[21] cried the countess, almost in tears, although she was protected by the choir stand and was in no danger.

The girls were also beside themselves from fear.

Several minutes later, order had been restored in the church. Again there was speechless, tense, reverent silence. All were listening greedily, holding their breath. Only occasionally could you hear the muffled, restrained wheezing of a short-winded old man or a baby's cry, but the mother rocked it so quickly and fearfully that it immediately quieted down.

---

[21] In French: "Lord, Lord, have mercy on us!"

25

The priest read in a slow singsong, drawing out his words as if he were reading from the Gospels. The decree was written in official, bookish language. The peasants listened breathlessly, but no matter how they strained to comprehend the document that was to resolve their question—to be or not to be—only individual words could be understood. The overall meaning remained dark to them. As the reading approached an end, the tense passion in their faces gradually disappeared, to be replaced by an expression of obtuse, frightened perplexity.

The priest finished reading. The peasants still didn't know whether or not they were free, nor, more important, had they an answer to the burning, vital question for them—to whom did the land belong now? Silently, with bowed heads, the crowd began to disperse.

The masters' carriage moved at a pace through the throng of people. Peasants scattered before it, removing their caps, but they didn't bow from the waist as they used to, remaining, instead, strangely, ominously, eerily silent.

"Count! Your grace! We're yours, you're ours!" a bold, drunken voice rang out suddenly through the general silence and a bareheaded fellow in a torn coat, who'd managed to get drunk during the service, threw himself at the carriage, trying to kiss the count's hand as he ran alongside.

"Get away!" A strapping young man with a dark, sullen face angrily pushed him away.

That evening, the entire Barantsov family gathered in the countess's small drawing room. Besides the immediate household and Mlle Julie, Auntie Arina Ivanovna and Uncle Semyon Ivanovich were also present. As a rule, they all spent the evening in different rooms, but today a sense of common woe had brought them together in a tight-knit group. Mama lay on her settee, complaining of a migraine, and Mlle Julie placed fresh compresses on her temples. Papa, sullen and lost in thought, paced around the room with his hands clasped behind his back. Uncle Semyon had taken refuge in a corner, breathing meditatively through his nose. Auntie Arina sighed loudly from time to time as she played solitaire.

A terrible snowstorm had come up toward evening. It sounded as if some living soul were raising a din in the chimney with a sad and prolonged howling. A gust of wind would suddenly whip in, the shutters would bang, and the metal sheets on the roof would crash. Each time, the countess shuddered and sprang up from her settee. The room grew darker and darker, and no matter how many times the lamp on the table was lit, it burned wanly and smoked: it was obviously in need of more oil, yet everyone pretended not to notice. All the servants had scattered, and no one wanted to get up to call a footman.

"The other day, the peasants at the Leskovskys' set fire to the manor house," Auntie Arina suddenly exclaimed.

"That comes as no surprise. There'll be more fires yet!" came Uncle Semyon's ominous croak from the corner. "Yes, a fine mess they've made!" he went on in his cheerless prophetic voice. "We'll see how this ends. Let's ask her," he said, pointing to Mlle Julie, "to tell us how it was in '89."

"*Mon Dieu! Mon Dieu! Que l'avenir est terrible!*"[22] Mama whispered nervously.

"Enough of this nonsense! A Russian peasant is no Jacobin!" Papa said calmly, to reassure her, but it was clear that the tone was forced and he was far from calm himself.

"Oh no, Michel, our peasant is a beast, our peasant is worse than the French!" In her agitation, Mama rose slightly from the settee, leaning on her elbow. "You know that the peasants hate us. . . ."

A door creaked in the next room. Everyone shuddered and looked around fearfully. Mama let out a frightened "Oh!"

It was Stepan arriving to announce that tea was served.

And now it was Vera's bedtime. There was no one in the nursery, and she opened the door to the hallway. She heard indistinct voices, the ringing of knives against plates, and peals of laughter from downstairs in the servants' quarters, where they were eating supper.

Vera had been strictly forbidden to run around the servants' quarters, but today she was forgotten. She was both frightened and eager to have a look at what was going on.

---

[22] In French: "My God, my God, how terrible the future looks!"

She stood racked by indecision for several minutes, but, since she was not of the timid sort, her curiosity got the best of her and she dashed downstairs to the cellar, where a feast was in progress. In the morning, the servants had been in a restrained, even somewhat dispirited mood: they were too afraid to believe. However, by evening their emotions had lifted: at supper, vodka had appeared from somewhere, everyone had a bit to drink, and restraint was thrown to the wind. Faces were flushed, eyes misted over, hair disheveled.

The smell of cabbage soup and rye bread, mingling with the heavy vapors of vodka and the pungent smell of cheap tobacco that stung the eyes, the discordant sounds of a concertina, the drunken voices drowning out one another—all this enveloped Vera as she came into the servants' quarters. Everyone suddenly fell silent and sat up straight at the young miss's appearance, but only for a moment. Soon the din started up again.

"Young lady, hey, young lady! Come on over here! Don't be afraid!" The coachman's drunken voice was heard. "Well, the masters are upstairs crying, no doubt? Are they sorry that they won't be able to tyrannize us anymore?"

"That's not true! Not true! No one's tyrannized you. Mama and Papa are kind!" The words flew out of Vera's mouth in a shout. In impotent anger, she stamped her foot on the floor. The Barantsov blood was aroused. She would have liked to hit, to throttle these shameless serfs. Indignation and insult drowned out her fear.

"They didn't tyrannize us! What do you mean? As if your deceased grandfather didn't maim a few people in his time! And why did he turn Andryushka the joiner over for army service before his time? Why did he send that girl Arinya out to the cattle yard?" several voices joined in at once.

The concertina stopped. All the servants crowded together, and stories began to pour forth about the good old days, stories that were disturbing, terrible, worse than any Vera had dreamed of, even in her nightmares.

"Well, that was Grandpa, but Mama and Papa are kind!" Vera wasn't shouting anymore: she spoke quietly through her tears, in a shamed voice.

There was a moment of silence. "Yes, the young masters aren't bad, they're kind," several people agreed, with apparent reluctance.

"Our master has grown tame lately, but when he was a bachelor he behaved pretty outrageously toward us girls," the old housekeeper, who'd had a bit to drink, observed spitefully.

"You are godless people! Sinners! You have no pity on a small child!" Nanny's angry, indignant voice rang out suddenly. She had noticed her charge's absence some time ago and had been running all through the house looking for her. It hadn't entered her mind to look for Vera in the servants' quarters.

Vera could not fall asleep for a long time that night. Novel, terrible, humiliating thoughts were troubling her. She couldn't explain very well what she felt so sorry about, or why she was so bitterly, so unbearably ashamed. She just lay in her bed and cried and cried. And below, from the cellar, she could still hear the stamping of feet, the discordant sounds of the concertina, and the drunken, incoherent yelping of a dance song.

III

After the emancipation, affairs immediately changed for the worse in the Barantsov house. The income from the estate dropped so precipitously that the entire household had to be shifted to a different footing. Though a decent fellow in the past, the village elder now turned into a scoundrel: again and again he was rude to the master, made difficulties about everything, and never delivered money on time. The count had to let him go and take on a new elder, but he was even worse. It seemed that almost every day, many old promissory notes and bills, signed by the count so long ago that he'd managed to forget about them, appeared out of nowhere. Upon seeing each new note, the count grew livid, shouting that it was forged, but he had to pay anyway. Soon he was obliged to sell both Mitino and Stepino, as well as the water meadows and the forest. Only Borki and an insignificant plot of land were left. The main woe was that now there were few buyers, and everything went for half its value.

Most of the household staff was let go. Those who remained had gotten used to being idle and lazy from childhood. Now they grumbled from morning to night that they had added work to do. Anger and being out of sorts became the masters' normal condition. They constantly quarreled among themselves too, but these quarrels had as much in common with their old ones as cold incessant autumn rain has with a good spring downpour. The count and countess now quarreled not out of jealousy but over money—nothing but money. Every time the countess came to request money for the household, the count rained reproaches on her for her extravagance, negligence, and the absence of order in the home. She could never order a new dress for herself or her daughters without a domestic scene. And if the count so much as mentioned a trip into town or to visit one of his neighbors, the countess immediately had an attack of nerves, not because she was wary of pretty young neighbors now but because she worried that her husband would lose at cards or squander their money in some other way.

Matters grew worse with each passing day. The count and countess were obliged to deny themselves one whim after another, but still there was not enough money and they just could not make ends meet. Like all impractical people, they tried to economize in the wrong places. They cut back on the most essential household items, worried about every bit of sugar or candle stub, but major expenditures remained unchanged. The estate manager, the village elder, the housekeeper, the cook, the coachman—all went on growing rich at the masters' expense. The only difference was that while in the past everyone had stolen with moderation and, so to speak, fairly, now the endless scenes, accusations, and reproaches made in vain against guilty and innocent alike and the eternal threats of dismissal embittered the servants; each was in a rush to grab as much as possible. As a result, the Barantsov wealth was dissipated with heat and rancor.

Everything about the household now bore an uncomfortable, miserly stamp. Under pressure from the daily corrosive squabbles and unpleasantness, both the count and countess abruptly let themselves go to seed. Later, when Vera recalled her mama, she always had an image of two women who did not resemble each other at all: one was young, beautiful, full of life—the mother of her childhood—while the other was capricious, quarrelsome, untidy, and intent on poisoning her own and others' lives—the mother of the later years.

The affairs of the Barantsovs' neighbors went the same way. Owners of estates had frittered away the earth under their feet. Now they stood by uncomprehending, helpless, at a loss as to what was happening to them. There was no thought of pleasures and amusements. When two or three landowners gathered together, they sat and bewailed their fates or unburdened themselves by complaining about the peasants and the government. In despair, the youngest and most energetic among them gave up managing their estates as a lost cause and left for Petersburg to seek posts. Only the old men remained in their country manors.

Lena and Liza Barantsova were now adult young ladies. Both languished from the tedium of country life and complained bitterly about their fate. Indeed, fate had played a mean trick on them. What had become of all their dazzling hopes? All their childhood and upbringing had been, shall we say, only preparation for that happy day when they would put on a long dress and enter high society. The day arrived, but it brought nothing but tedium.

Vera's life was not particularly happy either. The first budget-cutting measure undertaken by the Barantsov family was to dismiss all the children's staff. They found a plausible pretext for letting Mme Knight go, while Mlle Julie got bored and left on her own. Vera's parents decided that they could not afford to keep a special governess for her alone. The first gymnasium for girls had just opened in their provincial capital, but for the most part it was attended by the daughters of the town's minor officials, petite bourgeoisie, and merchants, and Countess Barantsova immediately took an aversion to the institution. The decision was made to send Vera to the Smolny Institute for Girls.[23]

---

[23] Catherine II created the Smolny Institute for Girls (also called the Smolny Convent) in Saint Petersburg in 1764.

Discussions about this ran on for almost a year, until the countess at last wrote to an old friend of hers in Petersburg, asking her to find out everything possible about entrance requirements. The response they received was both unexpected and vexing: Vera was already past entrance age.

The count now ordered Lena and Liza to devote themselves to their younger sister's education, a decision that did not suit the young ladies at all. "What did they train us to be, governesses?" they grumbled, taking to the task unwillingly. Vera, they said, was stupid, lazy, and slow-witted. Not a single lesson passed without tears. Both teachers and their pupil took every possible excuse to cut the lessons short. Since the parents on their part evidently soon forgot the unhappy question of their youngest daughter's education, her instruction gradually came to an end altogether. At the age of fourteen, Vera was left entirely to her own devices.

That summer, things were still tolerable. Vera spent entire days in the park on the estate, which had now grown wild, or she ran around the neighboring fields and forests. The peasants' children were shy of her, and, to tell the truth, she feared them no less. Whenever she passed through a village, it seemed to her that everyone was laughing at her in derision, and she began to feel a kind of instinctive animosity toward peasants.

Things went worse for Vera in the winter. She moped all day in one corner or another of the large, empty rooms without finding a thing to do anywhere. Bored, she started rummaging in the bookshelves, where she found only French novels, and by this time she had almost completely forgotten the French language, which she had spoken rather well at the age of five. The worst part of it was that everyone in the house was constantly out of sorts. No matter where Vera went, there was arguing, and she caught it from all sides. When she looked into her sisters' rooms, her sisters were always quarreling over some trivial thing, some finery they couldn't divide. If, contrary to expectation, they were on good terms that day, they most likely were complaining about their parents: "I daresay they didn't live like this when they were young. They've squandered their fortune, and now we have to stay in the country and be bored to tears." Coming to her mother, Vera would find her making a scene with a maid or the housekeeper. If she ran down to the servants' quarters, it was even worse.

In short, it seemed as if people were living only to torment and nag one another. The only person in the household who neither tormented nor nagged, who didn't even complain about anything, was the old nanny. She had but one worry on her soul: that the votive light in front of the icon in the corner of her room stay lit. Giving her a few kopecks to buy oil was enough to keep her happy and contented. This half-blind old woman, who had served the family all of her life, was allowed to remain in the house, but it seemed that people had forgotten about her: whole days went by without anyone's looking behind her partition, save perhaps a maid who remembered to bring her something to eat or Vera, her former favorite, who would stop by in the evening. Each time Vera entered her nanny's tiny nook, with its pervasive, distinct odor of incense, wood oil, and camphor, an amazing feeling of peace came over her.

"I'm so bored, Nanny," she would declare, dejectedly sitting down on the low chair and resting her head on the wooden table.

"Why, my precious, should you be bored? One must pray to God," Nanny would answer in the same placid, affectionate voice in which she had counseled Vera when Vera was, say, five years old. And indeed, heeding her nanny's advice, she began to pray fervently, passionately, in a kind of frenzy. Little by little, an enthusiasm for religion in its ritualistic, external aspect began to fill the idle, boring life of this child left to her own devices.

That year, Vera fasted very strictly for three weeks before Christmas. On Christmas Eve she ate nothing until the first star appeared. Accordingly, when the priests arrived, as they always did, just as twilight fell, and began reciting vespers before a temporary altar set up in a corner of the dining room, she felt a pleasant languor in all her limbs, as though she no longer had a body and would be able to leave the earth altogether at any moment.

The censers' blue smoke filled the room with a thick fog, through which the flame of the wax candles flickered. The pungently sweet smell of incense made her slightly dizzy.

"Peaceful light, holy glories," the choir sang, and it seemed to Vera that their voices came from somewhere far off.

"I need nothing, nothing on this earth, only to serve you, O Lord!" she thought, overcome by tenderness. Her heart overflowed with a miraculous, radiant joy, and an exalted sob tore from her breast.

A miracle occurred on that very day, or at least Vera regarded what happened to her as a miracle. Although her old nanny was illiterate, she had kept in her nook several books on religious topics that she regarded as sacred objects, occasionally asking her young mistress to read aloud from them. Among them was one called *The Lives of Forty Martyred Men and Thirty Martyred Women*. Once she had started reading, Vera was so taken by the book that she begged her nanny to lend it to her and spent whole hours absorbed in it.

"Why wasn't I born then?" Vera often thought with regret.

On that same Christmas Eve when she made a vow in her heart to devote her whole life to God, sitting alone in her former classroom, she suddenly noticed an old issue of *Readings for Children*, a magazine the family had once subscribed to for her sisters. With nothing better to do, she began leafing through it, and the first thing to catch her eye was a touching story about three English missionaries in China who had been burned at the stake by savage heathens. And to think this happened only five or six years ago!

So even now there were heathens in China! Even now one could earn a martyr's crown there!

"Lord, you've enlightened me. You've shown me the way, you've summoned me to a great feat!" In agitation and exaltation, Vera threw herself on her knees. In the fact that this old magazine had come to her notice precisely that day, as if in response to her heated prayer during vespers, she saw indubitable proof of God's providence. And, from that day forward, her fate was decided in her own eyes. All her dreams acquired a specific shape and direction. She now took a lively interest in everything concerning China, blushing at dinner whenever there was some chance mention of the country. Now, Vera had only one fear: that China might convert to Christianity before she was fully grown.

IV

The Barantsovs' house stood on a rise: to the north the hill sloped toward a large pond that had been dug out, of course, by the hands of Russian serfs. A garden in the Versailles style had been laid here with straight paths covered with crushed rock, flower beds in the shape of vases or hearts, and numerous arbors covered with jasmine, lilac, and linden. There was a time when this side of the house would have charmed the gaze of all admirers of manicured nature, but now that there was just one self-taught old fellow and two boys taking care of the garden instead of the previous gardener-artist working with a whole crew of helpers, it looked pitifully shabby. Slime covered the pond, which served as a breeding ground for countless generations of mosquitoes; the arbors had become rickety; and grass had pushed up through the paths. There is nothing sadder than a landowner's fanciful garden that has fallen into neglect.

The rear of the house, however, where fewer pains had been taken and nature had been allowed to take its own course, was quite lovely even now. A small oak grove stood alongside the house, and beyond it a hill dropped sharply to a stream that gurgled and frothed during high water but during dry spells was nothing more than a sand-filled ditch with a little rivulet trickling through it. The entire steep slope was overgrown with shrubs. In spring, it was covered by milky cherry blossoms, and the songs of orioles, robins, warblers, and other small birds filled the air: even nightingales came here at times. In fall, there were masses of nuts and wild raspberries, while in winter the slope was so blanketed with snow that it looked like a solid slanting white mass, with black twigs sticking out here and there.

The slope marked the boundary of the Barantsovs' holdings on that side of their estate. Land belonging to Stepan Mikhailovich Vasiltsev began on the other side of the stream. However, Stepan Mikhailovich had rarely troubled the count and countess until now, since he never lived in his manor. The doors on Vasiltsev's single-storied, wooden house had always been boarded and the shutters locked.

His neglected garden had become a shady green wilderness in which, under a canopy of old linden trees, the burdock had reached enormous, fabulous dimensions, and the fluffy pale heads of buttercups grew rampant alongside the small flowers of bluebells, pinks, and columbines grown wild.

Rumor had it that Vasiltsev was a very learned man. In the winter he lived in Petersburg, where he was a professor at the Technological Institute, while during summer vacations he usually traveled abroad. He had evidently quite forgotten about the small estate that he had inherited from his father. However, one day during this memorable winter, a post sleigh with bells ringing drew up before the Vasiltsev house: two gendarmes were sitting in it, with the manor's owner between them.

The matter was a very simple one. Vasiltsev had long had a reputation as a liberal and was regarded with hostility by many influential figures in Petersburg. That winter, on the occasion of some anniversary or other, the professors and students of the Technological Institute had organized a banquet, which the grand duke, who was the institution's chief patron, was to attend. His Highness let it be understood that it was not advisable for his path to cross Vasiltsev's. Of course, Vasiltsev was informed of the duke's wishes, but he responded that in that case he should be sent an official injunction stopping him from participating in the banquet, of which he considered himself, like all the other professors, to be one of the hosts. Of course, there was no injunction, and on the appointed day he calmly took his seat at the table along with his colleagues in the assembly hall of the institute.

Some two days afterward, the director of the secret police came to visit and cordially proposed that Vasiltsev put in for retirement and remove himself to his ancestral estate, without the right to leave it. To ensure his safety during the journey, he was provided with two guardian angels in gendarme uniforms.

These were the conditions under which Stepan Mikhailovich Vasiltsev was reinstalled on the paternal estate.

You can easily imagine the sensation that this event caused throughout the district. The most absurd, exaggerated rumors immediately began making the rounds about the new arrival and the reasons for his unexpected appearance. Many suspected him of being a dangerous conspirator, a suspicion that enveloped him in a mysterious aura that was at once both appalling and attractive, since even conservative Russians, unless they belong to the secret police, have an involuntary, instinctive respect for any political prisoner.

The Barantsovs were Vasiltsev's nearest neighbors, so it was no surprise that the two older girls, Lena and Liza, felt a natural sense of proprietary rights over this interesting, heaven-sent neighbor. He was a bachelor, although (to be quite honest) he could no longer be considered young, since he was past forty, and even less could he pass for

Adonis, but given the current paucity of eligible men, he could be considered a good match.

In all likelihood, Vasiltsev would have been more than a little surprised if told of the role he played in the two young ladies' conversations and plans. By some strange coincidence, throughout the following summer he could not leave his house without running into either Lena or Liza. What was stranger yet, they were always wearing whimsical attire or assuming exceptionally artistic poses. Either he would bump into playful Lena, who had climbed a tree like a squirrel and was looking at him archly through its dense foliage, or he would see a languorous Ophelia—that is, Liza—dreamily bent over the pond with a garland of forget-me-nots in her hands. If only you could have heard the graciously frightened cries of the young ladies when they were caught by surprise!

However, all these meetings came to naught. Vasiltsev would bow woodenly and coldly, then disappear. No conversation ensued, so it was no wonder that the young ladies finally came to the conclusion that the world had never produced such an ill-bred, uncouth bear as their neighbor.

While Vasiltsev's acquaintance with Lena and Liza went nowhere, it developed in a very straightforward, although admittedly far from poetic, manner with Vera.

Summer was coming to an end, and fall was beginning: rainy, muddy, with evenings that fell early. The forced, unfamiliar boredom of monotonous country life still often drove Vasiltsev outside the gates of his house to find distraction in long walks, but as would happen with anyone who hasn't lived in the Russian countryside, he often ran into difficulties and fell into great danger, or so it seemed to him.

In the professorial circles in which Vasiltsev had moved until that time, nobody would have suspected him of being a coward. On the contrary, his friends constantly trembled lest his inappropriate obstinacy put them in jeopardy. When his academic career came to such an unexpected end, even his most courageous friends sadly agreed that "It was inevitable. How could anyone as headstrong as Vasiltsev get by in Russia?"

In his heart, Stepan Mikhailovich considered himself to be a very bold man. In his secret dreams—those that you wouldn't admit even to a close friend—he liked to imagine himself in various unusual situations: more than once he had manned the barricades from the depths of his study. Nonetheless, despite his universally acknowledged valor, we must admit that Vasiltsev had nothing but the highest respect for the village dogs who, word had it, had bitten an itinerant beggar the previous spring, and for the village bull, who had already gored the cowherd twice. Vasiltsev did his best to avoid closer acquaintance with them.

On one occasion he had wandered a good distance from his house, leaving the main road. As usual, he was walking with head bowed and hands clasped behind his back, lost in thought and looking to neither one side nor the other. Suddenly, he found himself in a rather difficult predicament: all around him was a boggy meadow in which, whenever he veered from the narrow path, his feet sank up to his ankles in a muddy mess. Before him was a fairly wide stream, and behind him he could hear the tread and bellow of the village cattle.

"Hey, cowherd! Keep your beasts under control!" Vasiltsev thought to shout. But the cowherd, a boy of fifteen, weak of body and mind—he was sent to be a cowherd because he was of no use at other work—just mumbled something incoherent in response and cackled idiotically.

Vasiltsev stood there, racked by indecision, when all of a sudden he heard a young, almost childish voice, with a trace of laughter in it. "Jump across the stream! It's not deep, you know!"

He looked in the direction from which this kind advice had come and saw someone—was it a young lady or just a village girl?—about twenty paces away on a hill on the other bank of the stream. She was about fifteen, wearing a straw hat with a faded ribbon and a simple cotton dress that was too tight across her chest and too short in the skirt and sleeves.

Vera, who had also been driven to the spot out of boredom and, with nothing better to do, had long been observing this thin, amusing man who had so much diffi-culty with trifles. "Don't be afraid, jump!" she shouted again, but Vasiltsev could not make up his mind to do it. Vera then ran down the hill, fearlessly thudding in her old shoes through the boggy meadow, dragged a board from somewhere or other, and, with all her might, threw it across the stream, splashing her own white stockings and her neighbor's gray trousers with mud.

Now that he was out of danger, Vasiltsev was naturally quite ashamed of his cowardice. In confusion, he hurriedly thanked his rescuer and stood perplexedly in front of her, a forced smile on his face. Aware of the bad impression he had made, he did not want to go away immediately, but he hadn't the least idea how to strike up a conversation with this little savage who was staring at him with an adoles-cent's shameless curiosity.

"What's that book you're carrying? May I take a look?" Vasiltsev said when he had collected his wits. Under Vera's arm was her precious *Lives of the Martyrs*. Vasiltsev opened it at random and read the following: "Enraged at the virtu-ous martyr Isidor, Emperor Diocletian ordered the guard to take him to the Capitolium."

"What kind of nonsense is this?" Vasiltsev blurted out involuntarily.

Angry, indignant dark-blue Barantsov eyes flashed. Vera quickly seized her book, turned her back, and marched off toward her house without another glance.

Throughout the evening, Vasiltsev, against his will, kept thinking of that morning's comic episode: each time the memory provoked both laughter and a slight vexation.

The next day, without intending to, Vasiltsev returned to the scene of his previous day's disgrace. To his surprise, he found Vera there. She was standing at the stream with a look of thoughtful concentration on her face and seemed to be waiting for him.

"Hello," he said, stretching out his hand in a friendly gesture.

"Is it all really lies?" she asked instead of answering, raising her large eyes in a look that was now troubled and almost beseeching.

Yesterday, hearing that unflattering judgment on her favorite book, she was angry at first, but soon another, more painful feeling replaced her anger. "Everyone says that our neighbor is smart and educated. He must know all about these things. What if all that about martyrs is really just a fairy tale?" she thought. This doubt tormented her so much that she needed to clear it up no matter what the cost.

"Are you talking about the book?" Vasiltsev laughed. "Well, judge for yourself, young lady. Emperor Diocletian ruled in Byzantium, while the Capitolium is in Rome. How could he order the guard to take the virtuous martyr Isidor there?"

"Oh, so that's what you mean! Is that the only thing that's not true?"

"What do you mean—only? Isn't that enough?"

"Well, is it true that there were martyrs?"

"Of course there were."

"And were they slaughtered, burned, and set upon by wild beasts?"

"Yes, all of that happened."

"Thank God!" Vera exclaimed with a sigh of relief.

"Thank God they were tortured?" Vasiltsev asked. This eccentric girl was decidedly beginning to amuse him.

"No, not that, of course, not that," Vera rushed on in confusion. "I just meant to say, thank God that at least there were good people, saints, martyrs."

"But there are martyrs now as well," Vasiltsev pronounced seriously.

Vera stared at him in amazement for some time. "Ah yes, in China," she finally declared.

Vasiltsev laughed again. "No need to look so far away. Closer than that."

Vera continued to look at him, as her face reflected her growing incomprehension.

"Haven't you ever heard that here in Russia they arrest people, exile them to Siberia, and sometimes even hang them? How can you ask if there are martyrs?"

"But here they send only villains or criminals into exile!" These words flew out of Vera's mouth of their own accord. She had hardly uttered them when her face was covered by a deep red blush. "Our neighbor's been exiled," she remembered.

"But people are exiled for other reasons as well," Vasiltsev continued in a low voice.

They continued to walk along together for a while, in silence. Vera's head drooped, and she played nervously with the ends of her scarf. Strange, seemingly quite incongruous thoughts began to swarm through her head. She was terribly afraid of saying something stupid: suppose she were to insult their neighbor? But the matter was so important to her, so critical, that she couldn't stop considering it just for the sake of propriety.

"And why were you sent into exile?" she suddenly asked quickly, without looking at Vasiltsev.

He grinned. "Do you really want to know?" he asked, almost teasingly.

Vera just nodded her head in response, but her face spoke for her.

"So you want to hear about our contemporary martyrs too?"

Vera's eyes sparkled even more brightly.

"Would you like me to tell you? I must warn you in advance, though, we'll have to talk about a lot of other things as well." Vera's face was radiant. "And I suppose we'll have to talk about Diocletian and the Capitolium. Will you listen?"

"I will! I will!"

V

Vasiltsev came to call on Count Barantsov the very next day. The two of them quickly became friends, and when Vasiltsev expressed the desire some time later to give Vera free lessons, his proposal was accepted with gratitude, especially since the count, in spite of his apparently carefree attitude, felt pangs of conscience at times at the thought that the youngest daughter in the Barantsov line was being brought up as unburdened by knowledge as any village girl.

From that time forward, Vera's sisters had no doubt that she had charmed their neighbor, and they jokingly congratulated her on her conquest. Teasing Vera about her "suitor" soon became a habit with them. While at first the teasing conversations angered and confused her, little by little Vera began to find a certain fascination in them. Say what you will, but it's always flattering to hear that someone is in love with you. Vera felt more grown up and important even in her own eyes since she had acquired an admirer.

"Well, how did he treat you today? No proposals yet? Come on, don't keep secrets from us, please! Tell us everything!" her sisters pestered her after every lesson with Vasiltsev.

Vera, almost against her will, began to tell them and, also against her will, exaggerated a bit, although heaven knows how this came about! Her sisters could explain and decipher every word Vasiltsev said in such a way that it really began to seem quite different from what it was when first uttered.

Vera herself didn't notice how little by little her neighbor began to preoccupy her thoughts and her mental image of him was altered.

"A lanky, plain, not very young gentleman, his face the color of sand, and so nearsighted that even with his glasses he doesn't seem to see anything!" That's how she would have described him right after their meeting by the ditch. But now that he had become recognized as her admirer, she so wanted to make him into a hero that every day she discovered new virtues in him. One day she found his smile pleasant; on the next she noticed that when he laughed, funny, sweet wrinkles appeared around his eyes, and suddenly she would find those wrinkles terribly endearing.

Vera now lived in a state of chronic, unaccountable expectation. She got ready for every lesson with a pounding heart, and during the lesson itself she sat nervously, quivering in agitation. "Will this be the day?"

Vera and Vasiltsev were alone in the room. The lesson was over, but the teacher wasn't yet ready to leave. Putting his book aside, he settled down in an armchair, propped his head on his hand, and, as often happened, fell deep into thought. Vera sat motionless beside him. She turned her gaze to Vasiltsev's small, swarthy, thin hand and was mechanically examining a thick blue vein that began at the wrist, pushed aside several dark hairs, and, narrowing steadily, wound toward his middle finger.

It began to grow dark in the room: objects were gradually becoming dim, outlines fading. As Vasiltsev's hand was increasingly obscured in haze, Vera unconsciously strained to see it. She was overcome by a strange numbness, and minute by minute it became harder for her to move. Her heart beat with full, powerful strokes, and her ears were ringing, as if water were running somewhere far off.

Vasiltsev abruptly roused himself from his distraction. "Verochka dear . . . ," he began softly, as if continuing an earlier thought, and gently put his hand on hers.

"Here it comes!" flashed through Vera's mind. "Now he'll declare his love." But her nerves were too tense. Something suddenly tightened in her chest and rose to her throat: one word more, and she would suffocate.

"Please, please! Not a word! I know already!" a muffled cry tore from her. She jumped up and ran to the opposite corner of the room.

Stunned, Vasiltsev stared at her, for a few moments in silence and perplexity. "Verochka, what's wrong?" he finally asked quietly, timidly.

The sound of his voice immediately brought Vera to her senses, and it became clear to her that she had made a huge, terrible, foolish mistake. What should she do now? How could she explain it to him? "I thought . . . it seemed to me," she mumbled incoherently, gasping for breath.

Vasiltsev went on gazing at her, and an expression of unpleasant, irritated suspicion gradually replaced his look of frightened bewilderment.

"Vera, I want, no, I demand that you tell me what you were thinking!" He stood in front of her and held her hand tightly. His voice was stern and metallic, and his nearsighted blue eyes bore into her face. Vera felt that she was losing all her willpower and self-control under the effect of that fixed, inquisitorial gaze. She knew that confessing would be awful, but even if it were a question of life or death, she couldn't refuse to answer him and not tell him the truth.

She spoke at last in a barely audible, halting whisper, "I thought . . . that you were in love with me!"

Vasiltsev dropped her hand as if he'd been stung. "Oh Vera, you're no better than the others, just another silly young miss!" he said reproachfully, and left the room.

Vera remained alone, unhappy, devastated. "Lord! I'm so ashamed. How can I go on after such a disgrace?" This thought first occurred to her the following morning, after several hours of troubled, feverish sleep.

It was still early. She could hear the even, measured breathing of her sisters as they lay sleeping in their beds. They hadn't noticed anything yesterday, they suspected nothing, but what would they say when they found out? To have been the heroine of an interesting, absorbing romance for an entire month and suddenly to be proved a silly, arrogant girl. "I'm so, so ashamed!" Vera hid her head under the blanket and cried bitterly, convulsively, biting the pillow to muffle her sobs.

Lena rolled over in her bed. Her sisters were beginning to wake. "Just so they don't notice anything!" The thought quickly dried Vera's tears. She got up as if nothing were wrong, dressed, and throughout the day walked, talked, even laughed, as if nothing had happened. At times she actually managed to forget yesterday's incident for a moment, but in her heart a dull, unremitting, and entirely novel pain persisted.

Once more, the day fixed for a lesson came. "Something will happen now!" she thought, turning cold at the thought of meeting Vasiltsev, but at three o'clock a boy from the neighbor's manor ran over with a letter from the master: he was not feeling well and begged forgiveness for not coming to the lesson.

"Thank God," Vera thought with relief.

Vera now resumed the boring, idle life that she'd led before Vasiltsev. She moped about from one end of the house to the other, not knowing what to do with herself. No matter how hard she tried to hide it, her sisters suspected something and pestered her with humiliating, insistent interrogations. Vera tried her best to avoid their company.

One week passed in this fashion and another began, and there was still no sign of Vasiltsev. "He'll never come again," thought Vera with a sort of spiteful anguish. However, as she was sitting alone in her empty classroom one day, absentmindedly, without interest leafing through a book that she had already read some ten times, she heard familiar footsteps in the hallway.

Her blood rushed to her heart, and for a moment it seemed to her that it had stopped beating. Her first impulse was to jump up and run away, but before she could carry out that intention, Vasiltsev was in the room. He had the same quiet and kindly look on his face as always, as if nothing special had happened, as if these ten agonizing days had not even happened. And Vera? She had hated him so much during that week, but now a surge of mad joy suddenly swept her away. Of course, she was ashamed, painfully ashamed, but nonetheless joy dominated her feelings.

"Vera, my little friend. This cannot continue!" Vasiltsev spoke in a measured, gentle voice, as if addressing a child. "We've had a slight misunderstanding, a most unpleasant, vexing misunderstanding, but now we'll talk it out once and for all and then forget it and be friends as before. Verochka, I'm forty-three years old. I'm an old man, almost three times your age. You're closer to being a daughter than a wife. Falling in love with you would be not only foolish on my part but also base. Thank God such a thing never crossed my mind. But I do truly love you a great deal, and I really do want you to become a good person. Vera, only silly young misses imagine that a man can't be in their company for more than a half hour without courting them, but we know you're not one of those. Isn't that right?"

Vera stood silently, head down. Large tears quivered on her long eyelashes, but it didn't even occur to her to hate Vasiltsev at this moment.

"Listen, my friend, give me your hand," Stepan Mikhailovich continued. "To prove to you how much I value your friendship, I'm going to tell you something I haven't told anyone in a long, long time. Once I did really love a girl. I have never met a woman better or kinder than she. But she had an awful fate. This was right after Karakozov's attempt to assassinate the tsar, and everyone was being rounded up and taken in.[24] One careless word was enough to send you to prison, so she was arrested. The prisons were overflowing, and for six months she lived in a damp, dark cellar that flooded from time to time. And she was such a gentle and fragile creature! When the time finally came to sort out her affair, it turned out that there was no evidence against her, and she was released. But in that terrible cellar she had contracted an awful illness, the worst, surely, in the world—prison bone-wasting disease, it's called.[25] The illness destroyed the bones in her face. For

---

[24] The student Dmitry Karakozov was the first to attempt to assassinate Tsar Alexander II, in April 1866. After a lengthy investigation, he and thirty-five other radicals were brought to trial. What came to be known as the Karakozov Affair had an enormous impact in Russia and abroad. In chapter 9, Kovalevskaya addresses this affair in greater detail as she writes her own representation of a mass trial.

[25] Probably a form of osteomyelitis, an infectious, inflammatory disease that causes the death and separation of bone tissue. It is exacerbated by low temperatures and high humidity.

three whole years after her release she died a slow death. I, of course, never left her for a moment. Every day I had to watch this terrible, implacable disease disfiguring her, eating her up alive. Her sufferings were so great that even I, who loved her more than anything in the world, was moved to call death a blessed release. Now you understand, Verochka, that when a person has lived through something like this in his life, he can't take love lightly. To tell you the truth, in a country where things like this can happen, you hardly have the right to think about your own love and happiness." Vasiltsev's voice broke with emotion. Vera was sobbing silently and bitterly.

Shortly afterward, Vasiltsev showed her a portrait of his former fiancée made before her awful illness. Vera saw a swarthy, beautiful, and intelligent face with dark, dreamy eyes. It seemed to her that she had never seen a lovelier face. She touched the portrait reverently to her lips, as if she were kissing a martyr's icon,[26] and with tears in her eyes repeated her earlier child's vow to earn a martyr's crown. Only she wouldn't go to China for it. Now she knew that this crown was the lot of many in Russia.

From this day forward there were no longer any misunderstandings between Vera and Vasiltsev, and their friendship was sealed tightly and forever.

---

[26] It is customary when walking into a Russian Orthodox church to approach each of the icons (which would include those of saints and martyrs) and kiss them.

VI

It was the end of April. Spring came all at once that year, quite unexpectedly.[27] Cold weather had continued long after the rivers started to flow again and the snow melted. Everything moved slowly, sluggishly, almost unwillingly, one step forward, two steps backward. It was as if every plant and every blade of grass had to be coaxed and cajoled into casting off its winter's hibernation as it thrust the tip of a tender, chilly leaf out from underground. There was no real spring fervor to be seen anywhere. Suddenly one night, a quiet, warm rain blew in, and after that something magical happened. It was as if a yeasty ferment had scattered over the earth along with the finespun, fragrant drops of spring rain. Everything stirred, flaring up with the desire to prevail. Every living thing was in a hurry to move forward, pushing and crushing the others, as if afraid of being late. Each was determined to stand up for itself and its right to exist.

The inhabitants of Borki awoke the following morning in wonder at what had happened overnight. Garden, fields, and forests were all unrecognizable. The evening before, everything had been black, denuded, yet now it was all

---

[27] The nature description that opens chapter 6 can be read as an allegory for the era of reforms that followed Tsar Alexander II's ascension in 1855. The years of his predecessor, Nicholas I's, reign (1825–55) were often interpreted in the fiction and press of this period as winter's long dormancy followed by an unexpectedly intense, albeit uneven, pattern of reforms in the 1860s and 1870s.

covered with a light-green film. The air had changed from yesterday, the aroma was different, and breathing it was not the same.

At this moment the urgent, irrepressible fever of spring peaked. The birches were already bedecked in leaves as delicate and transparent as lace. The huge, swollen buds on the poplars dropped sticky, resinous scales that filled the air with a heady, intoxicating fragrance. Sweet-scented yellow pollen from alder and walnut catkins wafted everywhere, along with the white petals of the sweet and sour cherry trees. The firs sprouted huge, bright shoots, which stood upright like candles and stuck out oddly among the old branches, which were covered with last year's needles. Only the oak stood naked and sullen, apparently not even dreaming of spring.

New guests flew in every day from the south. Over a week ago, the first dark triangle of cranes was seen in outline against the sky. A woodpecker began tapping in the hollow of the old beech tree. Swallows dashed about under the roof of the balcony, searching for their old nests, and fought ferociously with the sparrows, who over the winter had seized their old domain.

The soil exuded warm vapors: it was as if you could sense some strange and mysterious work going on there below, in the depths of the earth. You couldn't take a step without treading on the germination of new, young life, be it mold, grass, or insect. In the pond, animated declarations of love poured forth. Every ditch also boiled with billions of the most varied and fantastic forms of life, all of it swarming and bustling, each thing imbued with awareness of the importance of its own existence.

A young lady of about eighteen, tall and shapely, with a delicate, flawless profile and thoughtful blue eyes rimmed with black lashes, sat bent over her desk in the former classroom of the Barantsov house. In front of her lay an open book—a volume by Dobrolyubov[28]—but it was clear that she was having trouble concentrating on what she was reading, since she kept lifting her head or leaning back in her chair. She began fiddling with the ivory penknife in her hands, and her eyes had a tense, expectant expression, as if she were listening for someone to arrive.

It would be hard to recognize in this young beauty the former swarthy, thin adolescent Vera. Three years had passed since her memorable conversation with Vasiltsev. Outwardly, those years passed quietly, with no major events or upheavals, but for Vera they were rich in inner substance. Her friendship with Vasiltsev continued to develop and grow stronger. But she somehow completely broke away from the rest of the family. Her sisters grew tired of teasing her on account of the neighbor and consequently

---

[28] The radical literary and social critic Nikolay Dobrolyubov (1836–61) was an associate of Nikolay Chernyshevsky and one of the "new men" who set in motion much of the discussion regarding reform in Russia in the 1860s.

lost interest in her. Because her intimacy with Vasiltsev began when she was still a child, her parents, in their usual irresponsible way, felt no need to interfere now that Vera was a grown young lady.

In the eyes of the neighboring landowners, however, Vasiltsev had recently committed several major offenses, so that his stock had taken a serious turn for the worse. First, he turned over to the peasants, without recompense, all the land on which they had previously paid quitrent, thereby not only causing significant loss to his own pocket but also setting a pernicious example for the entire district. Second, he was suspected of meddling in the affairs of others by giving the neighbors' peasants unsolicited advice: he had upset more than one cunning scheme contrived by some estate owner or other for the division of property with his former serfs.

In general, although no one could establish that Vasiltsev had committed any obvious violation of the law, everyone agreed that he was not behaving as a man in his position ought to and that he had evidently quite forgotten that a man exiled to his own estate for political reasons was obliged to proceed with particular caution. Some of his friends had already attempted to hint that the governor was beginning to bear a grudge against him, but he paid no attention to that either.

Although the estate owners grumbled about Vasiltsev, the peasants thought the world of him and were overjoyed whenever he appeared. It's true that at first they avoided him and even reacted with mistrust when he gave away his land. Then they decided that he must be a bit simple. Little by little, however, they became convinced that his actions could not be explained by foolishness. They saw that whenever they turned to him on any matter, they received aid or sensible, reasonable advice. From that time on, they besieged him. Whenever they needed to clear up some tangled family matter or write a petition to the court, a crowd of them would troop over to see him.

Vera spent her free time studying and conversing with Vasiltsev. Mostly, however, those endless conversations covered abstract topics that did not touch them personally. Just as they did three years ago, they often talked about contemporary martyrs; just as before—no, a hundred times more fiercely than before—Vera resolved to follow in their footsteps. However, the martyr's wreath lay ahead, at some point in the distant future, and for now her life was wonderful and became fuller and better each day.

The last few days, however, had been a bit boring and dreary: Vasiltsev was obliged to go somewhere to attend to a matter concerning the peasants. He had been away for two weeks. It was terrible how time dragged when there was no hope of talking to your friend in the evening. You didn't feel like doing anything, and no project went well.

But thank heaven, those days were finally coming an end! At midday a boy from the neighbor's estate ran over to say that the master had returned and would come to tea with them that evening.

"He'll be here in half an hour!" A rush of such strong and irrepressible joy seized Vera that she couldn't stay in her place. She threw her book aside and went over to the window. The slanted rays of the setting sun covered her with a fiery blush, making her blink quickly for just a moment.

"It's so lovely outside! I don't think there's ever been such an enchanting, wonderful spring! Look how everything's growing, it's all simply a miracle! This morning that hill was quite bare, and now you can pick off whole handfuls of cowslips and snowdrops. It's as if they crept out of the ground ready-made. There's a fairy tale about a fellow with such keen vision that he could see the grass grow. Well, in spring that's not so hard to do! I think if I looked closer, I could do it, too. . . . What's that? A cuckoo's call sounded in the forest. The first one this year . . . Lord, how lovely! It's so nice, your heart aches and you feel like crying!"

When Vasiltsev finally came in, Vera rushed to greet him so ardently that he lost his usual self-control. He took both her hands in his as he looked at her tenderly, in admiration. "What's happened to you, Vera? I didn't even recognize you at first. When I left two weeks ago you were a little girl, and now I find . . ." He didn't finish his thought, but his gaze said it all.

Vera blushed bright red and lowered her eyes involuntarily. It was so nice, so comforting to be with him. These two weeks had indeed brought about a change in her. Never before had her hands gone so cold or her cheeks blazed so hot in his presence. Mechanically, to hide her agitation, she started looking through the books on the table.

"No, Vera, we won't study today. Let's just sit like this for a while." He sat down near an open window and lit a cigarette. Vera sat down next to him. Her heart was beating very, very fast, just like that of a trembling bird.

It was already dark outside. High overhead, the sky was dark blue, but toward the west it grew gradually paler, and the horizon was edged by a light amber stripe. On the pond, frogs struck up a concerted chorus. In the corners of the room and on the ceiling, the thin whine of the first mosquitoes blended into a drawn-out, peaceful hum. A June bug flew past the window weightily, filling the air with its noisy, bass-toned buzz.

Something light-colored flitted by in the bushes that divided the kitchen from the garden. A woman with a scarf over her head stopped for a moment, caught in indecision. She took a sharp look around to see if anyone was following her, then quickly scuttled off in the direction of the wood. A minute later, a man's tender whisper and quiet, happy laughter could be heard. From the direction of the farm came the distant, plaintive sounds of a shepherd's pipe, played by the village virtuoso.

"Tell me about this business with the peasants. I heard so many awful, nasty things at dinner today," Vera began abruptly, but she evidently had to force herself to speak, and her voice sounded unnatural.

Vasiltsev shuddered, as if abruptly awakened. "Yes, I know that they condemn me," he said, passing his hand over his forehead. "But I've no doubt that I'll be able to sway public opinion in favor of these poor peasants. Vera, I'll tell you all about it in detail later. I can't right now!"

Several more minutes of silence ensued; only the mosquitoes droned and the shepherd's pipe started up again.

"Vera, do you remember one of our conversations, three years ago. I was so sure that this would never happen. . . . But in the meantime . . . Vera, tell me, do I seem like an old man to you?" The last words came out in a barely audible, tremulous whisper. Vera tried to respond, but her voice failed her.

The Lord only knows how Vasiltsev's hand ended up on hers. They both caught their breath at the touch, no words came forth, and both were afraid to stir.

"Stepan Mikhailovich! Vera! Are you here?" Liza's voice rang out in the hallway.

Vasiltsev quickly jumped up. "'Until tomorrow, Vera!" he said, stepping across the low windowsill into the garden and disappearing into the darkness.

The spring night, disturbing, fragrant, full of mysterious charms and passionate stillness, was afloat in the sky. The lights in the village had gone out, and all the sounds were gradually fading away. The shepherd's pipe had long since been silenced. The frogs had settled down, and even the mosquitoes were quiet now. From time to time there was a strange rustling in the bushes, something splashed in the pond, or a gust of wind carried from a distant village the plaintive howl of a yard dog languishing in solitude on this wonderful, passionate night.

Vera couldn't sleep. She was stifling in the large, cool bedroom that was now hers alone. Getting out of bed, she opened the window and held her hot cheek to the cold pane, but it didn't refresh her: her face burned as before, her heart was in the same sweet pain, and the same indistinct, blissful disquiet consumed her being. Everything was so still! At this hour, the grove seemed enormous and deep. The trees stood as tall and black as if they had come together to reach an understanding or to hide some strange, important secret. In the still of the night she suddenly heard a quiet reverberation: it was a post troika passing on the highway. The air was so clear, so transparent, that you could hear the clanging of its bells from as far as five versts away: there was a lull for a moment perhaps as the carriage went behind a hill, but soon it resounded again clearly, closer and closer. The troika was clearly traveling fast, at top speed. Now she could hear the crack of the whip, the voice of the coachman, and the horses' hooves. Then the sounds moved away again. Strange! It was as if they had suddenly been cut off: the troika must have stopped somewhere nearby.

Incredible, isn't it, that the sound of carriage bells can be so stirring at night! You know that nobody can be expecting anything of interest. Most likely, it's the government arbitrator or district police officer who's swooping down on the village to investigate crop damage. Nonetheless, whenever you hear that thin, silvery sound on the highway, your heart starts pounding and you feel suddenly an urge to be off, far away, to unknown lands.

"Lord, isn't life wonderful!" Vera folded her hands in a reflexive gesture, as if in prayer. Vasiltsev called himself a materialist, and Vera too was familiar with all the new theories and seriously thought that she no longer believed in God. But at this moment her soul was filled with a passionate, limitless gratitude to the Being that had granted her happiness. Old, indelible habit from childhood made her turn in fervent prayer to a God whose existence she did not acknowledge.

"Lord. I know that there's much sorrow in the world, much injustice, much need! I want to serve people, I'm ready to sacrifice my life for them. But Lord, only later, later. Right now I just want happiness, I want it so much, it hurts." Vera momentarily dropped off into a troubled sleep.

Vasiltsev's "until tomorrow!" bore through her consciousness like a bright beam, and again she was thrown into an agonizingly sweet disquiet, a hot, blessed fever.

Dawn had already broken and roosters crowed for the second time Under her window, the sparrows began to chirp loudly and worriedly—but Vera was still not asleep, tossing on her bed with burning face and icy hands. Only after the sun had risen did she finally fall into a deep, leaden sleep.

After that, however, she slept for a long time. It was late, almost noon, when again she was seized by a vague awareness that something incredibly fortunate had happened the day before. It was so wonderful to wake up on the day after a great, unexpected joy!

Vera lay luxuriating in her bed. "What am I doing, anyway? What about my children?"[29] suddenly occurred to her. She jumped up and was going to get dressed, but looking at her clock, she saw that it was so late, she had missed the lesson anyway, so there was no point in rushing. Having decided that, she went back to bed and closed her eyes, quietly smiling at the happiness looming before her.

Her maid came in, treading carefully and looking closely to see whether her young lady was sleeping. "Anisya, my dear, why didn't you wake me earlier?" Vera greeted her gaily.

"I came in at least five times, miss. You were sleeping so soundly that it seemed a shame to disturb you."

"Why does she look so strange today?" thought Vera.

"Miss, we've had a calamity!" said Anisya in that particular, excited, yet seemingly contented voice that servants always save for announcing important news, no matter what its character.

---

[29] Something is missing here: most likely, the author intended to tell us that, like any proper young radical of the 1870s, Vera is giving lessons to the village children.

"What is it?" cried Vera, jumping up on her bed. Although she had no idea of what had happened, her heart sensed a calamity to come.

"The police descended on our neighbor last night," Anisya informed her.

VII

The terrible news spread through the house like a clap of thunder. Last night a post chaise carrying a gendarme colonel and two guardian angels of lower rank had again pulled up to the porch of Vasiltsev's manor house. The colonel showed Vasiltsev a paper that bore an official stamp and seal. The document stated that Stepan Mikhailovich Vasiltsev, a member of the gentry, was an extremely dangerous person and a threat to the peace of the region. Thus, by the power vested in him, the governor proposed that he exchange his current place of residence for the excellent, although somewhat more remote, town of Vyatka. He was granted three days and three nights to settle his affairs, but at the end of that period the gendarmes were under orders to escort him to the designated location.

You can imagine the effect this news had on the whole Barantsov family! The count was more frightened than anyone else. He had that attribute, not uncommon in Russia, of expressing his discontent, playing the liberal, and wagging his tongue about the government behind closed doors, but whenever a dark-blue gendarme's collar appeared on the horizon, he immediately cowered and turned into the most humble and loyal servant of the tsar.

In this case, the count's inherent cowardice was made more acute by some well-earned pangs of conscience. How could he have permitted such intimacy between his daughter and this freethinker? Why hadn't he seen it? Yesterday Vasiltsev had been a respected, well-to-do landowner, an excellent match. Today all at once he was transformed into a homeless vagabond, a person too dangerous even to associate with. Naturally, there could be no question now of marriage between him and Vera. The girl had been compromised, shamed forever.

As was always the case when he was confronted by life's complications, the count rushed to quash any sense of his own responsibility by criticizing others. "You see, Mother, all you do is worry about your nerves! You couldn't look after your own daughter!" he reproached his wife. As for the countess, she was perfectly aware of the shame that had befallen the family as a result of the event, and she was already anticipating the pleasure of those innocent questions and expressions of sympathy that the province's ladies would shower on her at their first gathering in town.

The entire household, even the servants, was overcome by that particular, peculiar, inexplicable panic that the sight of the blue uniform is capable of provoking in Russia. Everyone expected some inevitable calamity. "The police are coming, the police are coming!" the servant girl Fenya ran in shouting once she heard the bell of the post chaise on the road. At that terrible news, all seemed to lose their wits from fear. The countess ran off to her bedroom, deeming her bed to be the safest refuge. The count ran to Vera's room, seizing books and papers at random, by the armful, and throwing them into the stove, which unfortunately happened to be lit. The servants all ran away God knows where. It turned out, however, that the alarm was groundless. It was just an excise official driving by, but none of them could calm down for a long while afterward.

As for Vera, the blow that had struck her was so unexpected, so overwhelming, she was stunned and could not immediately grasp the depth of her misfortune. That Vasiltsev had been taken away from her completely and forever—this was so unimaginably terrible that she could not quite accept the thought, or bring herself to think about what would happen after his departure. This "after" seemed to her a black, bottomless abyss that she could not look into without dizziness. Right now, her main concern, her most persistent, most tormenting fear, consisted of only one thing—he must not leave without bidding her farewell. To see him one more time, just for an hour, just for a minute—then let come what may! Sometimes it even seemed to her that if only they could see each other again, everything would be well, everything would sort itself out one way or another.

She now concentrated all her wishes, thoughts, and

aspirations on one objective—to meet with him. But arranging a rendezvous was difficult. Vasiltsev was, naturally, a prisoner in his own house, under strict surveillance by the gendarmes.

Vera, too, was under vigilant watch. Everyone in the family suspected she would try to play some kind of desperate trick. Therefore they put her under a form of house arrest also. During the day, her mother and sisters never left her alone for a minute, and Anisya was given orders to watch her at night.

Two days passed, and no matter how she strained her wits, Vera had not found a way to slip out of the house. She had received no news from Vasiltsev, since the servants had the strictest of orders not to permit even the dog from the neighbor's manor on the property. One night remained. Tomorrow Vasiltsev was to be carried off at dawn, and that would be the end of everything. Vera felt that the thought would drive her mad.

"Anisya, my dear one, sweetheart! Let me go to him. For an hour, just for an hour. No one will know," she begged the maid charged with watching her.

"Don't even think of it, miss!" responded Anisya, so frightened at first that she began flapping her arms in horror.

"Anisya, think of your youth! You used to tell me yourself how hard life was for you in the days of serfdom. And keep in mind that Stepan Mikhailovich is suffering because of you peasants."

"Oh, miss, you're ill, don't talk. Of course I know that he

was a kind master. Believe me, we servants are so sorry for him that we could cry, and for you too! We thought you'd make such a dear couple! It made us happy just to look at you. But what can be done? It's God's will! . . . Miss, what are you doing? Have you lost your mind, my sweet one? Falling to the floor at my feet, at a lowly servant's feet."

In despair, Vera had thrown herself to her knees before Anisya and was kissing her hands. "Anisya, if you don't let me go, know that my blood will be on your hands. I swear to you that I'll kill myself if I don't see him before he goes."

Anisya's heart was not made of stone. With many sighs and much lamentation, she finally promised to let her young mistress out by the back porch a bit later, when everyone in the house had gone to bed.

Night had already fallen when Vera, wearing Anisya's dress and a worn black shawl over her head, stole out of the house. It had turned cold again during the last few days; while the sun was warm during the daytime, by evening there was a light frost, so that the puddles on the highway were coated with a thin shell of ice that crunched under Vera's feet. A light shiver ran through her limbs. Since the stream that divided the two estates was now running high and had overflown its banks, it was impossible to follow her usual course across the ravine, so she was forced to make a detour of some two versts. Vera had never been alone in the fields at night, and the familiar road looked quite different to her than it did by daylight. Everything had suddenly changed and become unrecognizable.

She walked on without a backward glance, feeling neither fear nor agitation. Even her sorrow at Vasiltsev's pending departure had subsided. A slight, not at all unpleasant dizziness clouded her thoughts. Her legs felt surprisingly light, and she could not feel her body at all. As if she had been sleepwalking, she came to her senses only right before the gate to Vasiltsev's manor.

The house itself was dark. It was apparent that everyone was already asleep. There was only a weak band of light visible from behind the drawn shade of one window. Vera knocked at the gate, quietly and indecisively at first, but, when no one answered, she began knocking louder and louder. Two dogs sprang out from behind it and raised an ill-tempered, deafening barking. At last Vera heard steps. A sleepy gendarme wearing shoes over bare feet and his uniform coat thrown carelessly over his shoulders, came to open the gate with lantern in hand.

"What do you want? Who's that hanging around at night?" he mumbled angrily. "Oh, it's some kind of mam'selle. . . ." His vexation gave way to amazement.

"I need to speak with the master," announced Vera, in a muted voice. Her whole body was trembling, but she no longer felt at all timid.

The gendarme raised the lantern so that its light shone

right onto Vera's face and set about examining her, slowly and insolently.

"I guess it's a maid," he decided, speaking to himself. The confusion was disappearing from his face. "Well, listen, my beauty, you seem to know the road to the master's at night quite well!" he finally said with a grin. "But you see, tonight it'll be harder to get to him," he added, unexpectedly changing tone and becoming stern again.

"Let me in, for the love of Christ, let me in!" begged Vera. All she had understood from the gendarme's words was that she would not be allowed to visit Vasiltsev. She would have to leave without seeing her dear friend. Her voice was so beseeching, so full of despair, that the gendarme, who had a natural weakness for the female sex, could not resist.

"Now, now, don't howl!" he soothed her good-naturedly. "Let's see how we can be of service to you. . . . I'll still have to inform the colonel," he added, having given it a moment's thought. He let Vera pass through the gate, led her across the courtyard, and told her to wait in the hall while he went behind a partition to consult with the colonel, who had gone to bed but had been awakened by the noise.

The same numbness, the same utter indifference to everything that she had felt on the road again overwhelmed Vera. She was not embarrassed in the slightest when she heard the gendarme report to his superior that Vasiltsev's mistress had come to bid him farewell. She heard the colonel's off-color joke about her and his query as to whether she was a pretty wench. All this reached her ears without making the slightest impression, as if it had nothing to do with her at all.

"What the hell, let her in! Let him have one last bit of fun," the colonel finally decided. The gendarme opened the door to the inside rooms, and Vera flew in straight as an arrow.

"Now that's what I call burning desire!" laughed the gendarme. "But listen, honey, whatever your name is, don't forget about us next time, after your sweetheart leaves!" he shouted after her.

Vera heard nothing. In one breath, she ran through the two or three rooms that separated her from his closed door, through a crack in which a weak light shimmered.

Vasiltsev was sitting in the bedroom that also served as his study. He had not undressed as yet and was absorbed in sorting his books and papers. His large, spacious room now had that forlorn, untidy look that is usual before a departure. Linens, briefcases, and notebooks were heaped on the narrow iron bed, the blankets of which had been tossed into a corner. Scraps of paper, torn-up letters, and old bills lay scattered about on the floor. Two large wooden boxes were filled to overflowing with books, leaving the bare bookshelves along the walls looking like naked black skeletons. An open suitcase lay in the middle of the room, with linens, clothing, and a pair of boots poking out of it.

As she opened the door, for the first time since she'd left home, Vera was so agitated that for a moment she thought that her heart had stopped beating. She stood at the threshold, lacking the strength to take a step forward or utter a single word.

Vasiltsev was sitting with his back to her, bent over his desk, and so absorbed in what he was doing that he did not even notice the creaking of the door. However, when a moment later he chanced to turn around and saw Vera's tall, pale figure standing in the doorway, his face showed no surprise but only infinite joy: it was as if he had been waiting for her and was certain that she would come. He rushed over to her, and for several seconds they stood before each other, holding hands in silence, their throats constricted. With a suppressed sob, Vera threw herself into his arms.

Light steps could be heard behind the door, and the invisible presence of an outsider was palpable in the room. A nervous shudder, one of almost physical repulsion, shot through Vasiltsev's entire body. "Vera, my dear, calm down for God's sake. We're not alone. They're eavesdropping. We can't let these scoundrels gloat over our torment," he whispered through his teeth.

All his self-control unexpectedly returned. He took her by the hand and, pushing aside a whole heap of books, sat her down next to him on the divan. His face was very pale, from time to time a tic played at the corners of his mouth, and the blue veins on his temples were as taut as strings. But he began speaking in a calm and encouraging voice about extraneous matters.

"Here in this box, Vera, I've put aside the books I'm leaving for you. We started reading Spencer.[30] You'll find here some notes I've penciled in for you. . . ."

She sat on the divan without stirring, as if frozen in one position. Her hands were so tightly clenched that the nails on the fingers of one hand almost bit into the other. His words reached her as an indistinct hum with no specific meaning. When he turned to her with a question, she answered automatically, with a nod of her head or a weak, pitiful smile. She could not bring herself to speak, afraid that with her first word she would break into sobs.

The pendulum clock on the wall tapped regularly and distinctly. A large bumblebee whirred around the room, buzzing heavily and irregularly: it would quiet down for a minute and again start banging frenziedly against the ceiling and the windows. Vera had what seemed to be a physical sense of time dribbling away, like liquid from a broken vessel, drop by drop, fewer and fewer of the precious drops remaining. The separation, for many years, perhaps forever, was coming closer and closer. And yet not one heartfelt word, not one caress. Like strangers, they sat beside each

---

[30] The writings of the British positivist social philosopher Herbert Spencer (1820–1903) were popular, although often controversial, among Russian intellectuals in the second half of the nineteenth century.

other, and there was the same light rustling noise from the adjacent room.

The light from the tallow candle suddenly turned yellow. The window with the lowered shade, which before had appeared as a large black spot, now took on a bluish-violet tinge. Outside, a rooster crowed loudly, sparrows began chirping, cows began lowing—the usual harbingers of a spring morning in the countryside.

A cold, dull despair overwhelmed Vera. Now, for the first time, the prospect of separation loomed in all its palpable, hopeless reality. After all, until this moment there had still been the anticipation of the happiness of a final meeting. An irrational, inexplicable hope for something she could not even define was so strong that it had overshadowed the actual thought of parting. Now, nothing more remained, nothing. Everything had come to an end.

Vasiltsev got up from the divan, raised the shade, and opened the window. The first rays of a wonderful spring morning came pouring into the room. Light, noise, the spring fragrance of flowers, spring songs, everything came in at once—joyful, exultant, pitiless.

With a quick, inexplicable motion, Vasiltsev slammed the window and lowered the shade. He threw himself onto the divan and began weeping bitterly. All his tall, strong body shook from his sobs.

Vera leaped to his side. Dropping to his feet, she pressed against him with all her being and covered him with kisses.

"My sweet! My joy! Don't go away alone! My life! Take me with you."

Vasiltsev crushed her in his arms. No longer preoccupied with alleviating her pain, he now responded to her fervent caresses, pressing her close ever more firmly. Their lips met for the first time in a long, passionate kiss.

All at once, Vasiltsev came to his senses. He pushed Vera away sharply, almost rudely, got to his feet, and started pacing around the room. Alone on her knees in front of the empty divan, Vera continued to sob bitterly and noiselessly.

When Vasiltsev approached her again, his face suddenly looked pinched, as if after a long, difficult illness.

"Vera, my darling, forgive me!" she heard him say. "I've brought you so much grief, my poor dear! How could I take you with me? You, a fresh, young being—how could I chain you to this old, half-finished life? Even if I wanted to, do you think they'd let me? Wouldn't your parents have you forcibly returned?" His voice sounded dull and cracked. Vera was no longer crying. She knew the end had truly come.

Now it was completely light, and they heard a knock at the door. The gendarme had come to announce that they would be setting out in an hour.

"Vera, wouldn't it be better for you to leave now?" Vasiltsev asked in a quiet, muffled voice, but she silently shook her head. She wanted to remain with him until the end. That strange numbness, that awareness of the seeming unreality of everything around her, overpowered her again.

Vasiltsev too was walking and talking as if in a dream. One after the other all the members of his household—the old cook, the village elder, his peasant friends—began coming to bid him farewell. Entering the room, they first made the sign of the cross to the icons and then approached the master. After wiping their mustaches, they kissed him three times, seriously and solemnly, as if they were performing a religious ritual. Several women with babies in their arms stood by the porch, expressing their grief by wailing, as if in lamentation for someone who had died.

Vera looked on with dry eyes as these people entered, spoke, sighed, and wept. To her they seemed like automata involved in a strange and complicated performance.

The gendarme colonel was having a bite to eat in the next room and kept pouring himself something from a small decanter. "It wouldn't hurt you too, my dear Stepan Mikhailovich, to fortify yourself for the journey!" he exclaimed in a good-hearted, encouraging voice, furtively casting curious glances at Vera through the half-open door. He did not, however, address her directly, evidently having guessed that she was no simple chambermaid.

A tarantass,[31] harnessed to a troika, rolled up to the porch. The colonel got into it alongside Vasiltsev, as one of the gendarmes positioned himself on the box with the driver. The other remained in the house.

---

[31] A four-wheeled springless carriage.

"Heigh! Godspeed!" The horses took off, and the taran-tass, rocking from side to side, raced down the muddy road and was soon hidden at a turn beyond the birch grove. The sound of its bells grew fainter with every passing moment and finally ceased. There was nothing more to be heard, nothing except the usual melodic sounds of a spring morning in the countryside.

With bowed head, Vera looked straight ahead as she quietly walked back down the road. A flowering cherry tree covered her with white petals, and large, sweetly scented dewdrops showered her from its branches. A young hare sprang out into a glade and, sitting on a hummock, began drumming with his front paws to summon his mate. Catching sight of the human creature, he laid back his long ears and bolted into the forest. The sky sparkled and shone, as if the sun had dissolved in the azure heavens and engulfed the entire vault of the sky. From a dark, shimmering point high, high above her head came a powerful song of happiness and love that filled heaven and earth.

VIII

Time passed at a slow, uneventful pace. The days dragged on—monotonous, painful, full of leaden-gray anguish. At first, immediately after Vasiltsev's departure, Vera's whole organism was so shaken by the blow to her nerves that she did not even feel any strong sorrow. Whatever capacity she had had to live or to worry was now extinguished. She was stricken by a prevailing feeling of profound, overwhelming fatigue and spent entire days in a state of lethargy, incapable of the slightest mental effort. At times she would suddenly, unexpectedly, fall asleep during a conversation. This spiritual torpor was dissipated occasionally for an instant only by the memory, almost physically palpable, of her last moments with Vasiltsev. When she heard again his soft, caressing voice and felt the trace of his burning kiss on her lips, a passionate shiver passed through her body. It was strange, but after every such moment she suddenly felt an unexpected tranquillity, the unshakable certainty that it could not end like this, that they would see each other again.

With time, Vera regained her physical strength, but that only made her suffering more acute. As she returned to her ordinary preoccupations, the need to see Vasiltsev, a need that had been nurtured by three years of daily habit, made itself felt ever more insistently, more agonizingly. The least detail, the least trifle reminded her of him mercilessly, for he seemed to have left his stamp on all her surroundings. No matter what she did, no matter what she undertook, she would without fail encounter something that reminded her keenly of the past, of a happy moment, of some small, insignificant episode that she had practically ignored at the time, but the memory of which now provoked a burning rush of despair.

Worst of all was waking up in the morning. She had such strange, vivid dreams now. Vasiltsev's presence seemed so true to life that she felt his nearness with all her being, and everything happened so believably and was so endowed with a mass of small, authentic details, just like real life, that at times she said joyfully to herself in her sleep, "No, this is not a dream. This is true!" Then, as if a curtain had torn, for a moment everything began to spin, fade, and dissolve, a sharp trembling passed through her—and there was nothing left. Once again she was alone in bed; again she was seized by a tormenting awareness of her solitude; again she was lying there, convulsed and writhing with passionate, desperate sobs.

Vera's anguish grew worse and more persistent with every passing day. She had avoided her family before, but now the company of her sisters, their petty interests and empty talk, became unbearable. Everything seemed colorless or affected. Whenever she had to spend time with someone, all she could think about was getting away as quickly as possible. It always seemed to Vera that she needed to be alone, so that she could think seriously. As soon as she was left in peace, she indeed did set about thinking, or rather, daydreaming, hastily, fervently. The maddest, most far-fetched scenarios were sketched in her imagination. She mentally played out over and over the scene in which she would run away from home and search out Vasiltsev, wherever he might be, even at the bottom of the sea. These daydreams brought her momentary relief, but then a cold, sobering thought would arise from out of nowhere: "I don't have a penny, and it's three thousand versts to Vyatka. How far can you get in Russia with no passport?[32] At the first station they'll send me home under guard." Her daydreams vanished, leaving behind a bitter taste in her mouth.

There was not a sliver of rational hope. All that remained was an inexplicable belief that a miracle would happen. At first, when grief overwhelmed Vera, she felt it as a physical rebellion: "It is impossible to suffer like this! There *will* be an end." But there was no end. Her suffering became something normal and commonplace. Now, with each paroxysm of despair, the bitterness of the present moment was aggravated by the memory of the day before and the certainty that tomorrow would be the same.

But just when Vera had begun to succumb to hopelessness, when gloomy, dull, leaden anguish had become her permanent mood, there was the twinkle of a ray of happiness: she received a letter from Vasiltsev. He could not write her in the usual way by mail, since his letters would have been intercepted by either the police or her parents, but he contrived to send her a note through a friendly merchant who had trading interests in Vyatka.

The letter was short and extremely restrained, with no outpourings of tenderness. Clearly, Vasiltsev was aware that it could fall into the wrong hands. But it is unlikely that the

---

[32] Under Russia's passport regulations at this time, women were unable to obtain passports for either internal or foreign travel without the permission of their father or husband.

longest, most passionate epistle could have brought greater joy than that small scrap of paper. Vera was quite beside herself with happiness! As always happens when people have had more than their share of suffering, with the first hint of relief she was so quick to seize her joy that all her pain now seemed to be a thing of the past, and her grief nonexistent. The most important thing was to hear from him. The worst had been the feeling that he was totally lost, vanished into thin air, and that no ties to him remained. Now that there was the possibility of corresponding with him, his departure had become an ordinary one, and their separation a temporary unpleasantness rather than the previous, crushing, hopeless misfortune.

Although from the first minutes not only did Vera know Vasiltsev's letter by heart but also even the look of it had become etched in memory, not a day went by without her reading and rereading that precious bit of paper. She lived with this joy for a week after she received the letter and then became absorbed in waiting for the next one.

Like all people who are possessed exclusively by a single thought or interest and forced against their will to restrict themselves to a passive, temporizing role, Vera suddenly became terribly superstitious. She saw a good or bad omen in every trifle. She developed a childlike habit of trying constantly to guess her fortune. When she woke up in the morning, suddenly a thought would flash through her mind for no reason at all: "If Anisya comes into the room and says hello to me first thing, it will mean that everything will turn out well and I'll get a letter soon, but if, without saying a word, she first goes over to the window to raise the shade, that will be a bad sign." As soon as that absurd thought arose, Vera, agitated against her will, began to await her chambermaid's arrival with a racing heart and spent the day in a cheerful or sad mood, depending on the answer her oracle gave her.

Difficulties in corresponding notwithstanding, in the course of the summer and following fall, Vasiltsev managed to send Vera three letters. As he became convinced that his letters were safely reaching their destination, he began to write with ever more freedom and intimacy. His last letter was particularly tender and encouraging. He complained— true, just in passing—of a tenacious cough that he could not get rid of, but, in general, he seemed to be in good, cheerful spirits; for the first time, he began explicitly mentioning plans for the future.

"I am being given hope," he wrote, "that there will be an end to my exile. But even if this hope is not justified, in any case, in two and a half years you will be an adult in control of your own fate. My dearest child, if only you knew what crazy dreams your old friend, who loves you so madly, indulges in at times!"

Vera was beside herself from joy when she received this letter. She no longer doubted the future: two and a half years was not an eternity; they would pass, and then nothing, nothing in the world would keep her away from her beloved.

Alas! After this joyful letter no more came. As luck would have it, the friendly merchant went away on business for an extended period. True, he promised that his clerk would pass on Vasiltsev's letters while he was gone, but week after week went by and there was no news. Vera was now so firmly convinced of her future happiness that at first this absence of letters did not even disturb her very much: she found all sorts of reasons to explain it. But little by little her disquiet intensified and eventually became all-absorbing. Her thoughts focused exclusively on one thing: receiving a letter. During the day she kept listening for the merchant's messenger to arrive, while at night all she dreamed of was someone handing her an envelope bearing that dear hand-writing.

The torment of this fruitless, wearisome, incessant expectation became so unbearable at times that her whole being rebelled. Sometimes she felt bitter, even angry at Vasiltsev himself. "If only I'd never met him, I'd be living in peace now, like my sisters!" she thought with regret during these attacks of fainthearted weakness. Once, she was so overcome by a storm of contradictory, tormenting emotions that she tore up his most recent letter in a kind of frenzy, but the sight of the crumpled, torn-up white paper falling like snowflakes to the floor awakened a surge of repentance in her, along with a sense of self-loathing, as if she had raised her hand against what was dearest to her. She spent the next hour picking up the precious fragments and pasting them together on a piece of clean paper.

And again spring came, and still there was no news. In good weather, Vera went to the ravine, from which she could see the neighboring manor house, and sat for hours in dull, miserable apathy on an old, half-demolished bench.

Once, as Vera was sitting there as usual, she suddenly saw the post tarantass, which had turned off the highway and was heading toward Vasiltsev's house.

"What can this mean? Where is it going?" she thought, as her heart began to race. "Maybe it'll go by and on to the next village? But no, there it is clattering over the old, half-rotten bridge and turning down the neighbor's lane. There's no other road from there. . . . Lord, who could it be?"

The agitation overwhelming her was so strong that her legs began shaking violently and she barely had the strength to stand up. Her heart was pierced by a painful premonition, but at the same time a joyful shiver ran through her. "At least I'll know. Anything is better than not knowing!"

Quickly throwing a scarf over her shoulders, she ran toward the neighboring manor, but as she approached the house, Vera's steps involuntarily slowed bit by bit. Her heart contracted in growing pain.

The empty tarantass was standing in the yard, which was

now overgrown by grass. The coachman had taken off his hat and wiped the sweat off his face. Now he was busy with the horses. The front door to the porch, which had been boarded up for so long, was now wide open. Vera went into the hall, and then into the drawing room—it was empty. There was a damp, uninhabited smell. Light splashed weakly through the half-opened shutters. Furniture, chairs, tables, the divan—everything stood exactly as it had on the day that Vasiltsev left. The physical memory of that awful morning overwhelmed her.

The sound of voices came from the study as Vera walked in. The old yardman was at the window, busy with the shutters, which would not budge because the bolts had rusted. The former cook, carrying a large ring of keys, was drying her tears with her apron. In the semidarkness, Vera could barely make out three other figures sitting at the desk. One of them she finally recognized as the district police officer, while the other two—a man and woman in traveling clothes—were total strangers.

The shutter was finally opened, and now it was the officer's turn to recognize Vera. He came over to her. "Allow me to present the Golubinskys, relatives of our poor Stepan Mikhailovich. They received official notice the other day that their cousin died of tuberculosis in Vyatka. They arrived in our town yesterday and came to me so that I would turn over the property to them. By law, they inherit the patrimonial estate. . . ."

This time, nature took mercy on Vera: hearing the terrible news, she fainted. She developed a high fever and lay in delirium for several weeks. Her recovery was slow.

Little by little, however, Vera began to regain her grip on life, and like anyone who is recovering from a life-threatening illness, she now experienced a high degree of physical joy at being alive. With an instinct for self-preservation characteristic of those getting well, she distanced herself from all painful, serious thoughts. All her designs and desires were now focused on the trifling joys and sorrows in which the life of a recovering patient are so rich. These trifles assumed a strange, exaggerated importance in her eyes. Everything again took on for her, as for a child, the charm of novelty. She rejoiced if the broth was tastily prepared and cried if her pillow was not adjusted properly. It was a major event in the house when she was first allowed to eat a roast chicken wing.

When she had finally recovered and her life resumed its normal course, the past seemed quite distant to her, as if viewed through a smoky haze. Once, after she began to sit up in bed, her father brought her some papers to sign. Vera traced her name with a weak, trembling hand, but, having a premonition of something terrible, she did not even ask why her signature was needed.

It was only several weeks later, when she was fully recovered, that her parents informed her that Vasiltsev, on his deathbed, had made out a will leaving her part of his fortune. In gratitude, her father felt obliged to give Vera the letter that Vasiltsev wrote to her before his death.

"Vera, you were both daughter and beloved to me," he wrote to her, "and now, as I lie dying, I think only that you will be a continuation of me. I wasn't able to accomplish anything on this earth. I spent my entire life as an idle, useless dreamer. When I die, no trace will remain of me, like the grass in the field they speak of in songs—it's mowed and dried, and you can no longer see the spot where it grew. But you, my Vera, are still young, still strong. I know, I feel that you have been called to do something fine and exalted. What I only dreamed of, you will carry out; what I only had a vague presentiment of, you will accomplish."

Vera read these lines, written by a hand that had grown cold forever, with a veneration that overwhelmed her whole being. It seemed that a voice from the other world was speaking to her. She no longer experienced the earlier passionate, indignant despair, but she felt as if a black shadow now lay across her life and cut her off forever from the possibility of any simple, self-centered happiness.

Vera's illness seemed to shatter the routine of the Barantsov household and put an end to the long peaceful, boring lull. Changes rained down one after the other. The first change was of a very pleasant character, exactly the kind that the family had hoped and wished for: Lena became a bride. A new regiment was sent to their provincial capital, and one of its officers was the initiator of this happy change. However, the young couple had to leave soon after their marriage, since the regiment was being sent off to the other end of Russia. Liza, who was even more bored at home than before, went to join her sister in the secret hope of also finding a suitor among her brother-in-law's comrades.

In this way, the Barantsov family suddenly disintegrated and scattered to the four winds. The huge rooms of the manor house seemed even emptier than before. Then another unexpected event occurred, this one far from happy: the count suffered a stroke. Death only knocked at the window this time and passed him by, but it left indelible consequences: he lost the use of his legs, and his memory was weakened. He entered a second childhood. Propped up in his large, high-backed armchair, all day long he fussed and wept, demanding to be entertained, like a child. But the hardest thing of all for those around him was his mania for telling endless stories. He spoke for hours at a time, slurring and confusing words, repeating the same thing a hundred times, and becoming bitterly offended if no one listened to him. Vera alone had the patience to care for the sick old man and could understand his increasingly incoherent speech.

The countess, who had regained some of her cheerfulness on the occasion of Lena's wedding, was now completely dispirited and let herself go to seed. No longer paying heed to worldly matters, she became exceedingly religious, surrounding herself with God's people, monks and women pilgrims.

Vera, now obliged to be her father's nurse, could not even consider any sort of personal plan of action. Little by little, she fell into a resigned apathy. There was no foreseeable end to her present existence, since the doctors predicted that the count could live another ten years.

Fortunately however, that prediction did not prove true. After some three years, death came quite unexpectedly. One fine day, the count fell asleep more calmly than usual, and when Vera, surprised by his prolonged sleep, came to wake him, she found that he had turned cold.

The family came together for the last time for his funeral and then dispersed once and for all. The countess announced to her daughters that she had decided to enter a convent; the former estate manager bought the estate; and upon its sale each of the daughters received a sum of about twenty thousand rubles. Vera's older sisters returned to their lives as ladies of the regiment.

Vera was now completely alone in the world, fully her own mistress. Without giving the decision much thought, she went to Petersburg in quest of some kind of useful activity.

IX

During her first days in Petersburg, Vera experienced nothing but disillusionment. She became convinced that it was much harder to be useful than she had thought. In her eyes being useful meant either working personally for the

destruction of despotism and tyranny or supporting those
who worked toward that goal. She didn't understand that
one could be useful in other, very simple ways. But who
could she turn to for work that she would be fit for? Her
conversations with Vasiltsev, all of an abstract and idealized
nature, had ill prepared her for any sort of real action. At his
suggestion, Vera read a series of revolutionary publications.
In their talks, Vasiltsev presented a striking picture of all the
woes that humanity suffered, explaining that the root of
those woes lay in the fact that contemporary life was built
on oppression and competition rather than, as it should be,
on freedom and unity.[33] More than once he talked to her
about the martyrs to the cause—all those contemporary
heroes of freedom who sacrificed their lives and happiness
to bring about the triumph of this sacred goal. Vera came
to love these heroes passionately and shed more than one
tear over their fates. But in these conversations between
Vera and Vasiltsev no mention was ever made of what she
could do to follow in her heroes' footsteps, and in the years
of solitary reflection after Vasiltsev's arrest, she never

---

[33] The writings of major European socialist thinkers from Charles
Fourier through Pierre-Joseph Proudhon and Karl Marx were circulat-
ing widely in Russia in the second half of the nineteenth century.
Intense discussion of egalitarianism, capitalism, socialism, and democ-
racy was the order of the day. For an informative introduction to many
of the distinctive preoccupations of Vera's generation, see James H.
Billington, *The Icon and the Axe* (New York: Knopf, 1996) 359–472, and
Michael R. Katz's introduction to Chernyshevsky's *What Is to Be Done?*
(Ithaca: Cornell UP, 1989) 1–36.

stopped to ponder this question. She was always engrossed in contemplating the immediate task: breaking all ties with her family and leaving that tight circle in which she had passed her life. Her ignorance of the real conditions of life was so great that in her imagination the nihilists were something like a well-organized secret society working according to a definite plan to achieve clearly articulated goals. She had no doubt that once she arrived in Petersburg—that cradle of nihilist agitation—she would immediately be enlisted into the great underground army and take up a specific post in it, however modest it might be.

Such were her dreams through all those years. But here she was in Petersburg, fully mistress of her own life, free to do whatever she chose. But what did it matter? The goal before her was as unclear as ever. She didn't know whom to turn to or how to find those real nihilists. She was greatly disillusioned to discover that I personally did not know a single nihilist, and that I didn't even believe in the existence of a broad-based revolutionary organization in Russia. That simply hadn't entered into her calculations. She had expected more of me.

Nevertheless, I took it upon myself to advise her to enroll in lectures in natural sciences while waiting for something better to come along. The women's courses had just been instituted in Petersburg.

Vera took my advice and began to attend classes, but her mind was not set in that direction. She did not manage to catch up with her peers, nor did she share in their scientific interests. Most of her fellow students were younger women who worked diligently, with a specific goal in mind. They were trying to pass their examinations as quickly and as well as possible, so they could become teachers and live by their own labor. For the time being, all their interests were focused on their studies, and professors, courses, and practical training were the only topics of conversation. A sense of "universal malaise" was totally foreign to them. They were not averse to socializing when they had a free moment, and when the occasion arose—that is to say, anytime that male students joined them—they could not resist the desire to dance and flirt. All this, obviously, had nothing in common with the melancholy exaltation of a dreamer like Vera, and it should come as no surprise that even as she opened her pocketbook to them, she treated them like children and kept her distance.

Her studies were also unsatisfying. "There's still time to be involved in the sciences," she thought. "First I have to make sure that the main portion of the task is done." That was the spirit in which she answered all my attempts to persuade her to take her studies more seriously.

"I don't understand," she would say to me. "Given the woes that surround us on all sides, if we are sensitive to the sufferings that afflict humankind, how we can find satisfaction in examining the eye of a fly under a microscope, the exalted object, by the way, with which the good professor V. took up an hour of our time today."

Convinced that Vera had little taste for the natural sciences, I advised her to take up the study of political economy. The result was the same. Reading current tracts on political economy only wore her out, leaving no trace in her head. Even before she picked them up, she had decided that the task that preoccupied the authors—establishing the prosperity of humankind—would be achieved only when people shared everything among themselves and there was no longer neither oppression nor private property.

She regarded this as an unarguable truth, one that permitted no doubt and needed no proof. And, if that was the case, why should people perpetually rack their brains over wages, percentages, credit, and a whole series of similarly boring and knotty questions, whose sole purpose was to create a muddle in their minds and distract them from their real goals? These days, no decent person had the right to ask himself, "What aim shall I set for my personal life?" One could be interested only in choosing the shortest path that led to the achievement of the general goal. For a Russian, that could only be social and political revolution. And no textbooks on political economy could provide an answer to those questions. It followed, therefore, that there was no reason for reading them. That's how Vera reasoned with me.

Nonetheless, strange as it may seem, we became friends. We began to meet regularly, and a mutual feeling of sympathy permeated more than one conversation. I attribute this to the strange charm that distinguished Vera's whole personality. The features of her face showed such dignity, her every movement was so graceful and harmonious, and, most important, there was so much sincerity and naïveté in her behavior, that I set aside my reservations. It was impossible to argue with her, and all I could do was regret the underdeveloped mind that rendered her indifferent to all the great benefits of modern civilization.

As for Vera, I was her favorite acquaintance, but at the same time she couldn't understand how I had given myself up wholly to mathematics. She thought of a mathematician as a kind of eccentric who spent his time solving a riddle that expressed itself numerically. He could be forgiven this mania, since it was quite harmless, but it was difficult to refrain from a certain contempt for his weakness. And so, while each of us regarded the other with a whiff of condescension, this did not interfere with our mutual goodwill.

Meanwhile time passed, and Vera, feeling that she hadn't yet taken a single step toward achieving the goal she'd set herself, became ever more irritable and impatient. Her health began to suffer from the lack of fulfillment of this strange desire to "dedicate oneself to the cause." The bright blush began to fade from her cheeks, and the expression in her large dark-blue eyes became more pensive and sad with every passing day.

I recall a stroll we took along Nevsky Prospect one cheerful winter morning. The sky was clear and the sun spread its bright, sharp rays everywhere. One might think that some miracle had transported us to the radiant kingdom of Russian folktales. A silvery shimmer reflected off store windows, glistened under our feet, and scattered around us in tiny sparkles. The clear winter air was so refreshing that life itself became more cheerful. Passersby crowded us from all sides, and we could barely move despite the wide sidewalks. Men, women, and children with bright, rosy cheeks and with chins tucked into fur collars exuded health and good cheer.

All of a sudden Vera turned to me. "And to think that among these people there may be the very ones I've been seeking for so long. It's likely that there's more than one among them who could tell me everything that I have been trying in vain to find out. You know, every time I run across a likely looking person, I'm ready to stop him, look him straight in the eye, and ask whether he is one of them."

"Well, don't let me hold you back," I answered in the calmest possible tone of voice. "For example, look at that officer with the shining gold epaulets, or that foppish lawyer who's eyeing you so smugly through his monocle. Maybe you should start your questioning with them. Their appearance is promising." Vera just shrugged her shoulders and sighed heavily.

Something happened late that winter that immediately put an end to Vera's struggles and made it possible for her to find what she was looking for.

Since the beginning of January rumors had been circulating that there was a wave of arrests in various areas of

Russia and that the government had managed to uncover a cunningly conceived socialist plot. These rumors were soon confirmed: the *Government Bulletin* published an official report informing the state's loyal subjects that the justice system had detained an entire coalition of political criminals, seventy-five people in all.

––––––––––

A relative political lull followed the suppression of the Polish uprising, Karakozov's unsuccessful attempt to assassinate the tsar, and the exile of Chernyshevsky to Siberia.[34] True, even during that time a fair number of people fell under suspicion. Frequent arrests and exilings took their course, but it was impossible to identify a single general movement. The years of systematic assassination attempts had not yet begun. The very nature of revolutionary propaganda changed markedly, under not insignificant foreign influence. Earlier radicals had been consumed by the thought of political reforms and the overthrowing of the autocracy, but now socialist goals replaced them. The revolutionary intelligentsia gradually became convinced that,

––––––––––

[34] Between 1772 and 1796, the Austrian, Prussian, and Russian Empires partitioned Poland, and it lost its identity as an independent state. In 1830 and 1863 there were major rebellions against Russian rule. Nikolay Chernyshevsky (1828–89) was the most influential cultural figure and personality of the 1860s and in 1863 the author of the hugely popular novel *Chto Delat'?* (*What Is to Be Done?*). A radical journalist and advocate of enlightened utilitarianism, positivism, materialism, realism, and women's rights, Chernyshevsky was arrested in 1862 and spent the next twenty-one years in prison and exile in Siberia.

for as long as the common people remained ignorant and poor, it would be difficult to expect any substantive results.

To achieve anything, one needed to work among the people, seek a rapprochement with them, and share their simple life. This generation was best depicted by Turgenev in his novel *Virgin Soil*.[35] The seventy-five accused I mentioned above were among the naive but far from criminal propagandists. They were not armed with bombs or dynamite. Most of them came from good families, and their only crime lay in "going to the people." With this goal in mind, they dressed in peasant clothes and went to work in factories, with the secret intention of carrying out propaganda among the laborers. However, most often their activities were limited to frequenting taverns and markets, making revolutionary speeches, and passing out brochures to peasants.[36] Unfamiliar with the common people's mores or even with their ways of speaking, the propagandists carried out their mission so impractically and ineptly that, after their very first attempts to "produce ferment" among the workers, the factory owners and tavern keepers, often peasants themselves, informed on them to the police chief.

---

[35] Ivan Turgenev's last novel, *Virgin Soil* (1877), introduces a number of "populist" characters. The narrator's opinion of the novel was not widely shared by her peers, and *Virgin Soil* was strongly criticized by radicals, moderates, and conservatives alike.

[36] While information on the populists' failures in their efforts to "go to the people" was widely known, the narrator may also have based her description on material from Ivan Pryzhov's *History of Taverns* (1868), a unique history of proletarian life in the 1860s.

As slight as the practical results achieved by the revolutionaries were, the government, hoping to put an immediate end to any further agitation, nonetheless found it necessary to treat them with great severity. A decree was issued to detain anyone who fell into the hands of the authorities. To join the ranks of those suspected and be subject to arrest, all one had to do was dress in peasant clothes. Detainees were dispatched to Saint Petersburg for investigation and trial. Although most of them did not know one another, they were accused of being participants in a conspiracy, and that was what happened this time. The government wanted to make a strong impression both by the force of its retribution and by the severity of its justice. But although the matter was turned over for investigation not to a jury but to a special, government-appointed judicial commission, each of the defendants had the right to seek independent counsel, and the trial was to take place in open court.

Evidently, the government was not clever enough to take into account that in a country like Russia, with its vast distances and the absence of a free press, political trials were a fine instrument for propaganda. Many young people who shared Vera's convictions would not have found a way of "serving the cause" for a number of years if the periodic political trials had not shown them where to look for "real" nihilists. As a general rule, the defendants provoked lively sympathy in the most diverse circles. While direct relations with them were impossible, since in most cases they were kept under lock and key, one could freely approach their friends and relatives, and it was to them that people rushed to express their sympathies. Mutual trust was established between sympathizers and the objects of their sympathy: one supported and drove the other. That is why it comes as no surprise that after each political trial there was a re-enactment of that saying from the Russian bylina: "Ten come to take the place of one *bogatyr*."[37]

Vera too felt the influence of these political trials. After the first news of the forthcoming proceedings, she could think of nothing else. Every issue of the *Government Bulletin* became an object of diligent study. She knew by heart not only the names of the defendants but also those of their lawyers, and she rushed to take advantage of the first possible chance to become acquainted with the families of the accused.

That is how that broad field of useful activity she had dreamed of opened up for her. Seventy-five families thrown into poverty and despair by the arrest of their dear ones were in need of her assistance. She could actively help them, she could "serve the cause," and this gave her an opportunity to plunge into the milieu of people close to her in feelings and convictions. Needless to say, as soon as she became totally involved with her new friends, she immediately stopped attending classes or meeting with me. When

---

[37] The *bogatyr* was the larger-than-life hero of many early Russian epic tales (byliny) and songs.

she did occasionally drop by for a minute, it was only to enlist my assistance in the rendering of some service to those people dear to her. I would find myself either organizing a subscription to aid one or another of the victimized families, finding refuge for a homeless child, or convincing a prominent lawyer to take on someone's defense. In short, Vera was unstinting of both her own and others' labors.

The investigation was completed by the end of April, and legal proceedings began. A dense crowd was jostling at the doors of the courtroom by six in the morning. Only those who had passes could penetrate into the hall where the session was held. Others lined up at the entrance in hope of learning the verdicts as soon as possible. The public was allowed in at half past eight, and we unexpectedly found ourselves in a vast hall between two lines of gendarmes, who peered into our faces attentively as if trying to verify our right to be there.

A cursory glance was enough to tell me that the public was of two types. Some had come out of curiosity, as to a rare spectacle. These were for the most part people from good society who'd had no difficulty obtaining passes. Among them one could see ladies far beyond the first blush of youth and dressed in the black that good taste required. Many were carrying binoculars. Evidently, they were afraid of missing the slightest detail of the drama that was to unfold before their eyes. Their curiosity was so aroused that they were willing to sacrifice their habit of rising late and their natural fear of any contact with the common crowd. Almost all the men in this group looked to be of exalted rank, some in uniform, some wearing only a star.[38]

Everyone seemed to be frozen in expectation during those first moments, but soon the solemn silence was broken. Friends found one another and bows were exchanged. The amiability of the men expressed itself in their wish to cede the best seats to the ladies. Little by little, conversation started—first in whispers, then louder and louder. If this wasn't happening in the early morning amid bare walls and windows, on plain wooden benches, you might have thought that you were attending a social gathering.

Alongside this group of spectators there was another, composed of the relatives and close friends of the accused. Sad faces grown thin, worn clothes, a gloomy and leaden silence, glances fearfully directed toward the door through which the accused were to appear—everything about them spoke of the pitiful reality and the proximity of a cruel outcome.

At exactly ten a.m., the prescribed cry "Court is in session" rang out. Twelve senators[39] came in, all of them advanced in years, with more medals on their chest than

---

[38] Stars and medals were awarded to government civil servants in recognition of long or distinguished service.

[39] The senate was the highest judicial and administrative institution in tsarist Russia.

hair on their heads. Nevertheless, one could discern among them all the categories of Russian officialdom. Next to a self-important, complacent state servant who hadn't yet retired you couldn't help but notice a decrepit elderly man with a drooping lip and a semivacant look. Slowly, they took their seats in the armchairs with a certain solemnity.

Then a second side door opened and the seventy-five accused walked into the room escorted by gendarmes. These criminals had a strange appearance. Their emaciated faces contrasted sharply with their youth. The oldest wasn't yet thirty, the youngest had hardly turned eighteen. All wore their best, each with a different style of festive appearance. Among them were some young and pretty women. The agitation that gripped them gave their eyes a feverish sparkle and covered their cheeks with a sickly red blush. These young people had spent long months in complete isolation from the rest of the world. And here they were, unexpectedly brought face-to-face with their loved ones, recognizing their kin in the motley crowd of spectators. An irrepressible, almost childlike joy appeared on their faces. They evidently forgot the horrifying gravity of the approaching moment and the proximity of a sentence that would deprive them of every daily joy for many years to come. At this moment they remembered none of that: they only exchanged looks of joy and tenderness. In spite of the guard's efforts to stop them, many were able to shake hands outstretched to them and exchange a few words. Upon catching sight of them, their relatives and friends lost all self-restraint and threw themselves at the barrier with joyful greetings. I am convinced that no one who was in that courtroom will ever be able to forget that moment.

Even the ladies and gentlemen from elevated social circles, who had long since lost all capacity for strong sensations, were swept up in the general mood. For a moment their sympathies shifted to the defendants. Later, when they returned home and time had calmed their nerves, more than once would they blush at the memory of their involuntary enthusiasm, but now, at the present moment, they lost control of their emotions, and many of the respectable ladies waved their handkerchiefs at the sight of those terrible nihilists. But all this lasted only a minute, and the gendarmes soon managed to restore order and return the defendants to their seats.

The court session was in full swing, and the prosecutor read the indictment. In spite of the weight of the facts advanced in his speech, the defendants paid no heed to his eloquence. They looked at one another and tried to express their impressions, if not in words, then through signs. No matter how great the misfortune they had suffered or how frightening the fate that awaited them, at that moment they were as completely happy as if they had won a victory.

The prosecutor was a young man eager to advance his career, which explained his deafening eloquence. For over two hours he painted for the judges a dire picture of the revolutionary movement in Russia. With the boldness and speed of a botanist classifying plants in his herbarium by genus and species, he sorted the accused into groups, and within each found it possible to establish new subdivisions. He produced specific indictments for each category, but the most poisonous arrows of his eloquence were directed almost exclusively at five defendants. Two of these were women. One, the daughter of a high-ranking official, was very young, with a pale oblong face and dreamy gray-blue eyes. Her comrades called her "the saint." The other was older, sturdily built, evidently of rougher stock: her broad, flat face was not at all pretty and carried the stamp of fanaticism and obstinacy.

Among the men, one was a worker with an intelligent face, another a schoolteacher with all the signs of acute tuberculosis, and the third was a medical student, a Jew named Pavlenkov. It was he in particular who provoked the prosecutor's hatred and indignation.

Once he began speaking of Pavlenkov, the prosecutor could not restrain his fury and painted him as a true Mephistopheles. The other defendants were, undoubtedly, very harmful, he argued, and society was obliged to remove them for its own security, but one had to admit there were mitigating circumstances in their cases. However absurd the theories they preached, at least they truly believed in them, but one could not say the same about Pavlenkov, for whom revolutionary propaganda was only a means to advance himself and trample others in the mud. Nature had given him higher-than-average intelligence, but he had used this valuable gift only to cast himself and others into the abyss.

Following the example set by his colleagues in France, the prosecutor then described Pavlenkov's life from earliest childhood. He described him to us as a haughty boy who grew up with poor parents undeserving of respect. He argued that all moral principles were foreign to them, and since the parents had none, they were incapable of inculcating into their children that critical element without which the battle with depraved instincts is hopeless. A rich Jewish merchant, struck by young Samuel's intelligence, sent him off to school, where the boy studied diligently and successfully, but his studies failed to develop a sense of morality in him. After he received his diploma, the young man enrolled at the Medical Academy. This must have been an unexpected success for a poor Jewish boy, whose brothers and sisters still ran in the streets barefoot and ragged, but instead of thanking God and his benefactor, Pavlenkov nurtured and thrived on the anger that poverty and the humiliations of his childhood had first aroused. He was gradually overcome by an indomitable hatred toward everything and everyone above him, and he focused his mind and talents on gaining influence over his comrades, who had come from better families than his own. In his heart he cherished the thought of ensnaring them in his criminal designs.

The prosecutor continued in this spirit interminably. He finished his speech with the recommendation that the court punish Pavlenkov with the full force of the law. There could be no mercy for criminals like him.

While the prosecutor fulminated against Pavlenkov, I watched the face of the accused attentively. In a certain sense, he looked more interesting than the rest. He seemed older in both years and experience. It was impossible to find in him any trace of that childlike naïveté that emanated from the faces of the other defendants. He was dark-haired, with sharp Semitic features. His eyes were strikingly intelligent and beautiful, but a bitter, sarcastic, and at the same time sensuous smile distorted his mouth. His thick red lips clashed unpleasantly with the upper part of his face, which impressed one as delicate. The twitching of his facial muscles and the sharp motions of his hands testified to his tension. Of all the defendants, he alone displayed not the slightest joy at seeing his comrades, and no gazes wet with tears had met him when he came into the courtroom. Pavlenkov listened attentively to the prosecutor's every word and took notes from time to time, but not even the angriest outburst caused him to lose his composure. Were it not for the nervous twitching of his face, it would have been easy to take him for an indifferent, albeit attentive, observer with no personal interest in the outcome of the trial.

After the prosecutor's speech there was an hour-and-a-half recess. Both the visitors and the accused left the courtroom. The senators and defense lawyers hurried off to have lunch, and the spectators dispersed to neighboring restaurants.

When the court reconvened, the defense had its turn. Acting as a defense lawyer in a political trial is no easy matter. True, such a trial provided an excellent opportunity for advancement and making one's name. But all the lawyer had to do was display some fire and conviction in his defense, and he would immediately fall into the category of suspicious persons. Many still recalled that administrative exile could follow on the heels of an eloquent speech. However, we must say that, to the honor of the profession, there were always among the lawyers people selfless enough to put themselves at the defendants' disposal without the slightest hope of reward, as was the case here. Once again, people were found who willingly assumed the thankless and responsible role of counsel for the defense. Rather than protect their clients by denying their participation in the revolutionary movement, they contented themselves with portraying the motives for their clients' actions in the best possible light, developing bold theories and often expressing themselves in ways that would have been unthinkable in any but a political trial.

The presiding judge tried to interrupt them more than once, but all his efforts were in vain. A moment later they returned to their former manner and spoke their minds even more boldly and decisively.

The spectators grew more and more sympathetic to the accused. The society figures, who had come out of curiosity, listened in astonishment to matters that had never even crossed their minds. Their mentalities were as little attuned to this line of thought as were Vera's aptitudes in the opposite direction. Just as Vera regarded socialism as the only solution to all problems, these people accepted as an article of faith that the ideas of the nihilists were a form of insanity.

It was not surprising, therefore, that as they became acquainted with these ideas so eloquently expressed and saw that these terrible nihilists, far from being the monsters they had imagined, were, rather, unfortunate, totally self-less young people, a new world was opened to their eyes, and they no longer knew what to feel for the defendants. Their earlier contemptuous, sarcastic attitude evaporated. The sympathies that had gradually accumulated threatened to become enthusiasm. Only the judges continued to display their usual equanimity. The eloquence of the defense barely touched them. They had been given their instructions beforehand, and their verdict could be predicted. All that they showed were signs of fatigue and apathy from time to time. One could almost hear them grumbling, "So when will this come to an end?"

It was nearly evening. The presiding judge closed the session. The arguments would resume the following morning and continue again until nightfall. And so it went, day in and day out, for an entire week. Public interest did not diminish; on the contrary, it rose noticeably.

Pavlenkov's speech was clearly among the most brilliant. While it is true that he was not denied an attorney, Pavlenkov was not satisfied with his aid and took the opportunity to avail himself of his right to speak in his own defense. From the technical standpoint, his speech was incomparably less polished than those made earlier, but what gave it particular force and significance was its simplicity and lack of artifice. He ended by saying:

"The honorable prosecutor has told you that I am a poor, beggarly Jew, and he told you the truth: but it is precisely because I'm familiar with poverty and came out of the ranks of that despised nation that I sympathize with everyone who suffers and struggles. When I saw that I was powerless to do anything by the ordinary means, I decided to turn to extraordinary ones, without a thought as to whether or not they were legal. The honorable prosecutor has told you that in view of my humble state I should be punished more severely than the others: let it be so, let them do anything that he wants. I will not seek your compassion, since I belong to a race that is used to suffering and patience."

At the end of the arguments, the judges retired to settle on a verdict, but the spectators remained in the courtroom. When the senators returned to their seats about two hours later, a solemn presiding judge quietly read the verdict, which took about an hour. Most of the defendants were sentenced to exile in Siberia or distant provinces. Only the five felons I mentioned before were sentenced to hard labor for terms varying from five to twenty years. As expected, Pavlenkov was given the maximum sentence.

In government circles, the verdict was unanimously regarded as lenient. Everyone had expected harsher sentences. However, the spectators in that courtroom did not agree. The verdicts came as a rude, stunning blow. During that week, the people had lived as one with the defendants, had gotten to know each of them personally, and had probed into the innermost aspects of their past. Therefore it was difficult for the spectators to remain indifferent to the fates of the accused, or to see the situation as readers of a newspaper so often do when they learn of an irreversible calamity that has befallen a person unknown to them.

As soon as the reading of the verdict was finished, a deadly silence, broken from time to time by sobs, reigned in the hall. My gaze involuntarily shifted to Vera. She stood, holding the railing, white as a sheet, with eyes wide open and that uncomprehending, almost ecstatic expression you encounter on the faces of martyrs.

The crowd began to disperse slowly and wordlessly. Outside, spring was at play: water was flowing off the roofs and coursing down the sidewalks in fast-moving rivulets. Clean, fresh air filled our lungs, replacing the miasmas of the courtroom. Everything that we had lived through those past days seemed only a bad dream: it was difficult to believe that it had all really happened. As in a fog, I could see those twelve impotent old men who had experienced all of life's joys a long time ago and now, in tranquillity and satisfaction, pronounced a verdict that cut off at the roots the happiness and joy of seventy-five young beings. Surely, anyone could see the bitter irony in that.

X

Several weeks went by. There was no sign of Vera and no word from her. For my part, I kept intending to visit her but somehow never found the time. Then, one day at the end of May—I had invited guests for dinner and we had just gotten up from the table—the living room door suddenly opened and Vera came in. Only, my God, how she had changed! I couldn't help but cry out in surprise. All winter she had worn a kind of black, shapeless garment, a "monk's cassock," as I jokingly called her costume, but today she unexpectedly appeared in a light-blue summer dress, fashionably styled and belted with a silver Caucasian sash. The dress was extremely becoming, and she looked some six years younger. But it was not just the dress. Vera's whole mien was sparkling, triumphant: her cheeks were rosy, and her dark-blue eyes sparkled, flashing fire. I had known before that Vera was pretty, but I had not suspected until now that she was in fact a beauty.

Most of my guests were seeing her for the first time and Vera's entrance into the living room caused a real sensation. Not only the men but the ladies as well were struck by her beauty and crowded around her before she had even had a chance to sit down.

In the past, when Vera dropped in on me by chance and encountered a stranger, she immediately took refuge in a corner, and you would not get a word out of her. Unsociable by nature, she instinctively avoided anyone new, especially if she suspected that the person would not be sympathetic to her ideas. Today, however, things were totally different. Vera was in a kind, benevolent mood and treated everyone affably and graciously. It seemed that a great joy was coursing through her, overflowing her being and flooding everything that surrounded her.

In the past, Vera abhorred being paid compliments, but today she listened to them tranquilly, with a certain haughty grace, brushing them aside gaily, glibly, and so cleverly that I marveled watching her. Where did all this come from? Her worldliness, her wit, her coquetry! This, you see, is what blood means. You think she's nothing but a nihilist girl, but then just look—a sophisticated young lady!

This extraordinary spectacle did not, however, last long. Vera's animation suddenly seemed to snap. Her garrulous- ness disappeared, and a blasé, scornful expression appeared in her eyes.

"Will your guests leave soon? I need to speak with you about something serious," she whispered in my ear. Fortunately, the guests began to disperse.

"Vera, what's happened to you? I wouldn't recognize you," I asked her as soon as we were alone.

Instead of answering, Vera showed me the fourth finger of her left hand, on which, to my utter astonishment, I noticed a smooth gold ring.[40]

"Vera, are you getting married?" I exclaimed, astonished.

"I already have! My wedding took place at one this afternoon."

"But how can that be, Vera? Where's your husband, then?" I asked in confusion.

Vera's face lit up. A blissful, exalted smile played on her lips. "My husband's in the fortress. I married Pavlenkov."

"What? But you didn't even know him before! How did you manage to get acquainted?"

"We're not acquainted at all. I saw him from afar at the trial, and today, a quarter of an hour before the wedding, we exchanged a few words for the first time."

"What? What does this mean, Vera?" I asked, not understanding. "Did you fall in love with him at first sight, the way Juliet did with Romeo? Maybe while the prosecutor was tearing into him at the trial?"

---

[40] An odd detail, since Russians normally wear wedding rings on the fourth finger of the right hand.

"Don't talk nonsense!" Vera interrupted me sternly. "There can be no talk here of falling in love, neither on my side nor on his. I simply married him, because I *had to*, because it was the only way to save him!"

I looked inquiringly at Vera in silence. She sat down on a corner of the divan and began telling me her story, without haste or agitation, as if she were speaking about completely simple and ordinary matters.

"You see, after the trial I had a long talk with the defense lawyers. They were all of the opinion that the situation was far from bad for all the defendants, except Pavlenkov. Of course, the schoolteacher will die in two or three months, but he wouldn't have lasted very long in any case, since he has acute tuberculosis. The others are all being sent to Siberia, but we can count on their returning to Russia, once their sentences are finished, to take up the cause again. That is not what's in store for Pavlenkov, however. His lot is definitely a sorry one, so sorry, that it would almost have been better if they had sentenced him to be shot or hanged. At least everything would be over quickly, but to spend twenty years suffering in hard labor!"

"Well, Vera, it's not as if he's the only one ever sentenced to hard labor!" I remarked, timidly.

"Yes, but you see there are different kinds of hard labor. Had he been a common criminal rather than a political one, and if the prosecutor hadn't tried to make such an example of him, it would have been a different matter. He would have been sent to Siberia, and that wouldn't have been so bad. People do manage to live in Siberia, and there are so many political prisoners there now that they are a force in their own right: the authorities have to take them into account. Now, if someone is sent to Siberia, he's not too distressed, knowing that while things will be hard there, in time matters will sort themselves out and he will find like-minded brothers and sisters. He won't be totally cut off and needn't lose hope. And if anyone feels too miserable, with any luck he can flee. After all, more than a few people have escaped from Siberia.

"But the government has found a means of coercion that is worse than exile. For political criminals of the highest category, the most dangerous ones, there's the Alekseev ravelin in the Peter Paul Fortress.[41] If the government wants to finish off people, they send them to hard labor not in Siberia but to that damnable pit. It's right in Petersburg, under the noses, if you will, of the highest authorities. There can be no thought there of tolerance or indulgence for prisoners, only the strictest regimen of solitary confinement. Anyone who ends up there might as well be buried alive. No visits with other convicts, no letters from friends, and prisoners are forbidden to send out any news about themselves. A person is erased from the ranks of the living,

---

[41] Situated on the Neva River in the heart of Saint Petersburg, the Peter Paul Fortress was the favored site of incarceration for well-known political prisoners, including Dostoevsky; Chernyshevsky; and Alexander Ulianov, Vladimir Lenin's brother.

that's it. Our government doesn't stand on ceremony, but even so it won't do to sign too many death decrees, it's embarrassing: what will they say abroad? So they devised this Alekseev ravelin. It sounds better than the gallows, but the result is the same. So many political prisoners have been sent there already, but you never hear of a single one coming out. Usually, a few months go by, or at most a year or two, then the family is informed that the person in question passed away in peace, lost his mind, or committed suicide. They say that no one has ever survived more than three years in the Alekseev ravelin. And this was the cursed dungeon awaiting Pavlenkov."

Vera halted, all pale from agitation. Her voice trembled, and tears hung suspended on her long eyelashes.

"But how did you manage to save him?" I asked impatiently.

"Wait, you'll find out in a moment," continued Vera, calming down a bit. "As soon as I learned of the fate awaiting Pavlenkov, I can't begin to tell you how sorry I felt for him. Morning and night, I couldn't get him out of my thoughts. I went to his lawyer and asked, 'Can't we do anything for him?' 'Nothing,' he said. 'If he were married, that would be a different matter, there might still be hope! You know, the law says that a wife, if she so chooses, can follow her husband into hard labor. So, if Pavlenkov had a wife, she could appeal to the emperor, stating her wish to follow him to Siberia. The tsar, not wanting to deprive her of her legal right, might possibly have mercy. But unfortunately, Pavlenkov is a bachelor. . . .'

"You understand," continued Vera, again falling into a quiet, matter-of-fact tone, "as soon as I heard those words, what I needed to do became clear: petition the tsar for permission to marry Pavlenkov."

"But Vera!" I exclaimed. "Didn't you give a thought to the consequences such a step would have for you? You don't know what kind of man this Pavlenkov is, whether he's worth such a sacrifice."

Vera looked at me with a stern, astonished look. "Can you say that seriously?" she asked. "Don't you understand that if I didn't do everything, absolutely everything, in my power, I would be contributing to his destruction? Tell me, in good conscience, if you weren't married, would you really not do the same?"

"No, Vera, to tell you the truth, I don't think I could have done it," I answered frankly.

Vera looked at me intently. "Then I feel sorry for you!" she responded, then continued: "In any case, it was clear to me that my duty was to marry him. But how could I get permission to do so? That was the catch. When I informed his lawyer of my decision, at first he declared that it was a preposterous thought—they would never allow it. I myself had no idea how to proceed in the matter, but suddenly I remembered that there was one man who could help me. Have you ever heard of Count Ralov?"

"You mean the former minister? Who hasn't heard of him? They say that even now, though he's distanced himself from affairs of state, he's still close to the tsar. But what ties can you have to him?"

"Well, you see, he's a distant relative, but that's not all. The critical thing is that he was once in love with my mother, yes, and it seems, in earnest. When I was a little girl, he often used to bring me candy and carry me around in his arms. Of course, until now it didn't occur to me to remind him of my existence—what had I to gain from people like him? But now I realized that he could be of use, so I wrote him a letter to ask for an audience. He immediately replied and set a time for me to come."

"Well, Vera, quickly, tell me how things turned out!" I said, my curiosity piqued. "I imagine that you must have taken the old man by surprise. He must have been overjoyed to see his former favorite." I remembered everything I had heard about the old count, how he turned pious and now spent his days fasting and praying. The meeting between him and Vera must have been an odd one, and I began laughing involuntarily at the thought.

"There's nothing to laugh at, it's not at all funny," Vera said, offended. "Just you listen to what a clever girl I can be, what brilliant ideas sometimes occur to me," she continued merrily. "Do you think I would go to see him dressed as a nihilist? Nothing of the sort! I know that all these old sinners, even though they spend their twilight days fasting, can't resist a pretty face. As soon as they see a comely little mug, they're moved, they melt and can't refuse her anything. So I put on my best to go see him: actually, I even ordered a dress made for the occasion," Vera pointed to her outfit in self-satisfaction. "I affected such a very modest demeanor, you would have thought I was as meek as a lamb.

"So the count set our appointment for nine o'clock in the morning, and I went. I must tell you, those great lords know how to live! Someone who's donned a monk's habit, taken vows of humility, and wants to atone for his sins has no business living in such palatial quarters! A fierce-looking doorman holding a mace and looking like a lord himself met me at the entrance. At first he didn't want to admit me, but I showed him the count's letter, at which point he struck a copper gong on the wall. At that moment, out of nowhere, a strapping haiduk, all covered with gold braid, appeared. He escorted me up a marble staircase lined with flowers. At the top, another strapping haiduk met us, conducted me through some formal rooms, and handed me over to a new footman dressed in livery. I was led me from room to room and from drawing room to drawing room. Parquet floors with marquetry shone like glass everywhere. They were so slippery that you would fall headlong if you didn't watch your step. The ceilings were covered with murals, there were mirrors in gilded frames on the walls, the furniture was covered with damask and gilded. It was all empty—not a soul in sight. And the footman was so self-important, he walked silently, without uttering a word. . . .

"At last they brought me to the count's own study. Here the count's personal valet received us. The other footmen who had escorted me earlier were all stately and wore gold-embroidered livery, but this one was a little old man, wretched to look at, in a simple frock coat that looked well worn, although his face was intelligent and sly—that of a real diplomat. He looked me over intently, from head to foot, as if trying to penetrate my very soul. Then slowly, oh so slowly, he said 'Madam, you will wait here. His Highness the count has just arisen and now deigns to pray.'

"I was left alone in the study. The room was enormous. It seemed that from one end you could not see at all clearly what went on in the other. But here there were no mirrors or gilding, just simple oak furniture and dark drapes and curtains everywhere. Even the windows were half covered, and I was immersed in semidarkness. An enormous icon case, with several votive lights burning in front of it, completely filled one corner of the room.

"I sat and sat there. The time dragged terribly. Still the count didn't appear! My impatience finally got the best of me and I began to listen more attentively. From behind a drape it seemed that I could hear an indistinct mumbling. I quietly lifted a corner and caught a glimpse of another room, which was all upholstered in coarse black cloth, so that it resembled a Catholic chapel. There were icons, crucifixes, and votive lights everywhere. In the corner stood a small, feeble, mummy-like old man. He was whispering something, continually making the sign of the cross, and bowing to the floor. He was supported on both sides by two enormous footmen, who would lower him to his knees and then stand him up again, just like a spring-loaded doll. ... One of them was loudly counting, keeping track of how many times His Highness had deigned to bow to the floor that day.

"Watching them was so amusing that I lost my timidity. Only when the footman had counted to forty did it evidently suffice, and the count was conducted away from the icon screen. I barely had time to drop the drape and assume a modest pose when His Highness appeared before me.

"As soon as he saw me, he exclaimed, 'Lord, it's Alina (that was my mother's name), the very image of Alina!'[42] His eyes filled with tears. He began to bless and make the sign of the cross over me, and I kissed his hand and tried to wring a tear from my eye as well.

"Touched to the heart, my old fellow began reminiscing about the past, and, since I'm no fool, I imitated his tone, saying nothing about my business but telling him various fairy tales about how my mother always remembered him, prayed for him, and saw him in her dreams. I really haven't the slightest idea how I came up with it all so quickly.

---

[42] Kovalevskaya forgets that in chapter 2 she named Vera's mother Mariya. Alina is a diminutive form of Elena.

"His Highness softened up completely, just like an old tomcat when you scratch it behind the ear. He began to promise me all sorts of blessings and to make plans on my behalf. He almost contemplated presenting me at the imperial court! You know, there was a moment when he was ready to adopt me as his daughter, since he no longer had any family of his own—his wife and children were all dead.

"Now I saw that the time had come. I burst into tears and told him, 'I love a man, and the only thing in the world that I want is to marry him.'"

"Well, and how did the count receive this confession?" I asked with a laugh.

"Oh, not badly. At first he was sympathetic—he started comforting me, trying to make me stop crying, and he promised to work on my behalf. But when he found out who I intended to marry—well, that was another story. The old fellow flew into a rage, refusing to hear another word. His tone changed from tender to formal. He stopped calling me sweet child, angel, and shifted to madam. 'If, madam,' he said, 'a well-brought-up girl happens to fall in love with an unworthy man, only one option remains to her parents: to pray to God to enlighten her.' I could see that things were not going well, and I was in utter despair."

Vera broke off.

"Well, and then what happened, Vera? Finish your story," I persisted.

She blushed. "To tell you the truth, I myself don't remember everything that happened next and what I actually said to him. It's just that . . . that all at once he got the idea that I *had to* marry Pavlenkov to cover my sin and save my honor."

"Oh, Vera, weren't you ashamed to fool the old fellow that way?" I cried out reproachfully.

Vera glanced at me in surprise. "Fool the old fellow that way," she mocked me derisively. "As if that's something to be ashamed of. And he, isn't he ashamed? With his position and the influence he has on the tsar, how much good he could do, how useful he could be! And what does he do? Beats his forehead on the ground, in the hope that maybe in heaven he'll be given the same kind of warm little place he had here on earth. He has little concern for anyone else. He was loving toward me, but why? Because my little mug was to his taste: it reminded him of old sins and stirred his old blood. A lot of thanks he deserves for that. And what about the rest of our young people who are perishing, rotting in Siberia: does he treat them well? Not on your life! How many sentences has he signed in his lifetime? Would I be trying to fool him if I could talk to him as one human being to another? But that was impossible. If I had come and simply said to him, 'Save Pavlenkov,' he would have answered, 'Madam, stay out of matters that don't concern you,' and that would have been the end of it." Vera's self-control failed her, and her face turned bright red from agitation.

"Well, go on, please go on," I urged her along. "What happened then?"

"So, at first he was horribly angry. He started pacing around the room, and, as is always the case with old men when they are upset, he began mumbling to himself so loudly that I could hear: 'Unhappy child! To take leave of her senses like that! From such a fine family! She's not worth making a fuss over, but for her mother's sake I'll have to save this wretched girl. Somehow we must cover this sin, so the whole family isn't besmirched.'

"He walked around the room, mumbling, while I listened, barely restraining my laughter, though I had to keep up my grief-stricken look. I sat there, losing hope and not daring to raise my eyes, just like a Gretchen,[43] that's all.

"At last he stopped before me and said sternly and imposingly: 'Sit down, Vera, and write to the tsar immediately that you are throwing yourself on his mercy and you beg permission to marry your unworthy seducer. I will take it upon myself to deliver your petition and see that the affair doesn't become public.'

"I began to thank the old fellow, but he pushed me away. 'I'm not doing this for you,' he said, 'but for your mother's sake.'

---

[43] Gretchen is the nickname for Margaret, whom Faust seduces in the first part of Johann Wolfgang von Goethe's poetic drama of the same name (1808). Russians, including Lev Tolstoy in *Anna Karenina*, often used "Gretchen" to refer to a young, innocent woman of good breeding.

"I sat down to take his dictation, but now I saw that there was another obstacle. He was dictating the words for my petition, but without a word about Siberia. 'What about Siberia?' I asked. 'I will follow my husband to Siberia.' The old man burst out laughing. 'They won't demand that from you. Your sin will be covered by marriage, and you can live wherever you please afterward, as an honest widow of sorts.'

"I must tell you that hearing those words really frightened me. What should I do now? I was afraid to insist too much on Siberia: suppose this seemed suspicious to him and he guessed what was really going on? I just didn't know what to do. But then I got a bright idea: I told him that I repented and wanted to take this deed on myself as an act of contrition and follow my husband to Siberia to atone for my sin! Well, this my old fellow could understand, it was more in his spirit.

"Deeply moved, he said that he would not stand in my way. 'It is in God's hands,' he said. In parting, he even blessed me, taking a small icon off the wall, and hanging it around my neck."

"Well, and what happened then?" I asked.

"And then, everything fell into place by itself. I returned home without saying a word to anyone about where I had been. Less than a week went by before my landlady came running in, all red and out of breath, to give me a calling card. She was so agitated that she could hardly speak: 'A general has come to see you, a very imposing man! He sent

130

a footman in livery upstairs to inquire if the young lady is at home, he needs to see you. He's sitting down there in his carriage, waiting.'

"I read what was on the card: *Son excellence le prince Gelobitsky*, and on the bottom, in pencil, was added, *de la part du Comte Ralof.*[44] Well, I guessed immediately what business he had come on. 'Ask him in,' I said. Now my landlady lost her head altogether. 'Oh saintly fathers, what will I do? The general is so refined, and your room hasn't even been cleaned. And to make things worse, I'm cooking cabbage soup for dinner today. You can smell the cabbage all over the house, heaven forbid!' 'Well,' I said, 'that doesn't matter! The general will know that we eat cabbage soup. Ask him in anyway.'

"Now I could hear him coming up the staircase, which is dark, narrow, and old, and it squeaked under his feet. From time to time his saber got caught in the banisters. All the children in the house came running out of their rooms: not daring to come close to him, they stood there, some sticking their fingers in their mouths, others in their noses, looking at the general as if he were a wild beast.

"The general came in. He was not yet old, middle-aged, something of a dandy, with a long mustache streaked with gray and sticking straight out, evidently pomaded. He reeked of perfume. He had probably never been in such a

---

[44] In French: "His excellency, Prince Gelobitsky. From Count Ralov."

setting in his life, but being a sophisticated man, he gave no sign that it was out of the ordinary. The landlady hastily offered him a wooden chair with padded arms. He, as if noticing nothing, sat down as familiarly as if he'd been in some society drawing room, placed his helmet on his knees, stretched one leg out in front, and turned to me with an amiable smile, saying, *'C'est bien à la princesse Vera Barantzof que j'ai l'honneur de parler?'*[45] 'Yes,' I replied, 'that's me, the very one.' He waved his hand, signaling the landlady to leave us alone, bent toward me with a confidential look, and said that he had been sent to me by the tsar himself to find out whether it was true that I wished to marry the political criminal Pavlenkov and follow him to Siberia.

"'Yes, it's true,' I answered.

"Now he began to reason with me. How could such a fine young lady, such a beauty, ruin herself? Had I thought of what I was doing? I, a Russian noblewoman, marrying a converted Jew, a state criminal! My children would have neither name nor title! They would surely reproach me when they grew up!

"'I've given this a great deal of thought,' I said. 'I won't change my mind.'

"The general could see that I was standing my ground.

---

[45] In French: "Is this indeed Princess Vera Barantsov with whom I have the honor of speaking?"

He contorted his face into a kind, fatherly grimace and even winked at me. Bending toward me, he took my hands and began whispering, 'I'm not a young man, I have children of my own. I will speak to you as I would to my daughter. Anything can happen to young lasses! You're not the first and you won't be the last! It's not worth ruining your life because you've done something rash. The emperor is merciful, and the count is well-disposed—he's prepared to do a lot for you. Even if there was a sin, it can be covered up: we'll find you another husband!'

"I continued pretending that I didn't understand any of that and persisted with my own argument: I wanted to marry Pavlenkov, and I wanted to follow him to Siberia.

"The general saw that he could do nothing. He got up, bowed, and left, and I went to Pavlenkov's lawyer, told him everything, and said, 'Go right away to your client and inform him of the plan we've come up with to save him.'

"A few days later, a document arrived, permitting me, Countess Barantsova, to enter into lawful wedlock with the state criminal, the Jew Pavlenkov, after he renounced Judaism and converted to the Orthodox religion, and we would be married in the prison church." Vera became silent and thoughtful. We sat for several minutes without saying a word.

"Vera," I finally said sadly, "the deed is now done, and it's too late for regrets. You've thrown yourself into the maelstrom. But please have the grace to tell me why you never came to see me before your wedding and never said a word to me about what you were taking on. After all, we considered ourselves friends!"

Vera hugged me and laughed. "What an odd thing to expect!" she pronounced merrily. "As if someone who's throwing herself into the maelstrom would not do so heedlessly! What do you think? When a person decides to hang himself, before he puts his head in the noose, he should make the rounds of his friends and ask their blessing?"

"So you admit that you've thrown yourself into the maelstrom?" I asked quietly.

"You see," Vera pronounced, having paused to think. "I'm not going to pretend or play a role with you. I'll tell you frankly. At the moment when that document came and I saw that all the obstacles had been cleared away and my goal achieved, I should have been overjoyed, but no, suddenly I felt anxious. And there was still a week before the wedding! I kept dreaming up all kinds of work and business, just to be in motion constantly and avoid thinking at all. As long as I was out and about during the day, I was all right, I put up a brave front, but as soon as night fell and I was alone, it was simply misery: my heart would begin to ache and I'd get the jitters.

"I went to the prison today. They let me in. The heavy, iron-clad door slammed behind me with a bang. It was warm outside, the sun was shining, but here I was suddenly enveloped in darkness, and there was a damp smell. I was terrified. It occurred to me that I had left behind my happiness, freedom, and youth on the other side of that door. I even had a ringing in my ears, and I suddenly felt as if I were being stuffed into a black and bottomless sack.

"I showed the document to the person in charge. They led me down some endlessly long corridors. Two gendarmes walked with me, one ahead, one behind. From the side doors, figures in uniform kept popping out to eye me from head to foot with brazen curiosity. The entire prison staff must have known about the upcoming wedding, and everyone wanted to take a look at the bride. With no shame, they made various comments about me. I heard one officer saying loudly to another, '*Ces sacrés nihilistes ne sont pas dégoûtés, ma foi! C'est vraiment dommage d'accoupler un beau brin de fillette comme ça à un brigand de forçat. Passe encore, si l'on avait le droit du seigneur!*'[46]

"His comrade replied with something I couldn't understand, probably an obscenity, because suddenly both of them guffawed loudly, rattled their spurs, and, passing me, stooped down to look insolently right into my face, so close that their enormous mustaches almost touched me.

"With every step, my heart contracted more and more. I honestly confess that if someone had arrived at that

---

[46] In French: "These damned nihilists have no scruples, the devil take them! Truly, it's a pity to hitch a fine slip of a girl like that with a convict. It wouldn't be so bad if at least I could have the first pass at her."

moment and proposed that I renounce the wedding, I would have gladly run away without a backward glance.

"At last, they brought me into an empty room with bare, painted walls and two wooden chairs for furniture. They left me there alone, with instructions to wait. I don't know how long I sat there, but the time seemed endless. Doubt— had I done the right thing?—kept crossing my mind. Was I not doing something terribly, unforgivably foolish? And most horrible of all was the thought of my upcoming encounter with Pavlenkov. I was afraid that I might not even recognize him. And what would he say to me? Did he understand me? I attempted to call up his image as he had appeared to me in past days, but no matter how I tried, it was all in vain.

"Finally, I heard steps, the door opened, and two gendarmes brought in Pavlenkov. What he looked like, the features of his face, I still can't tell you. I only remember that he was wearing a gray convict's coat and that his hair was closely cropped. The policemen stepped aside, pretending not to watch as they gave us several minutes alone.

"What took place between us I remember as if in a dream. I think that Pavlenkov took my hands and said, 'Thank you, Vera, thank you!' His voice broke off, and I too couldn't find anything to say. The only thing is, if you can believe it, from the moment he walked into the room, all my torment passed. My heart became light and clear. My doubts all vanished. I knew now that I had done the right thing, that I couldn't have done anything else. We were escorted to the church, positioned side by side, the priest took our hands and began to lead us around the icon table. All this too I remember foggily now. At one point, a billow of fragrant smoke wafted from the censer, and when the choir burst into 'Rejoice, Isaiah!,' I even fell into a state of distraction for a bit. At that moment it seemed to me that it was not Pavlenkov standing beside me but Vasiltsev, and I could hear his dear voice clearly and distinctly. I know very well that he would have approved and been overjoyed watching me. And suddenly everything became clear to me: my entire future life unrolled in front of me, like a map. I would go to Siberia, make a life among the exiles there, I would comfort them, serve them, and send letters home for them."

Vera's voice broke, and she began to sob. "And to think that I moped about all last winter looking for work to do," she said in a voice that now sounded cheerful and joyous. "But it was here, right at hand, and what work it is! I couldn't have thought up anything better. I can tell you in all honesty: I probably would not have been any good at anything like revolutionary propaganda or conspiracy. For that you need a great mind, eloquence, the ability to affect people, to bring them under your leadership, and I have none of that. And I would always have been racked by regrets for putting others in danger. But going to Siberia—that's just the thing for me, real work! And it's all so simple, so unexpected, as if it happened by itself. Lord, I'm so lucky!"

She threw her arms around me, and for a long time we exchanged kisses and cried.

Some six weeks later, I stood at the Nikolaevsky railway station seeing Vera off on her long journey. Immediately after their wedding, Pavlenkov was sent to Siberia as part of a group of other convicts. They were to make most of the journey on foot. Now the time had come for Vera to set out as well, so that she could meet her husband at their destination. She was not traveling alone: two other women were with her: one had a daughter, the other a husband among the exiles. Naturally, they were traveling in third class, but this was still a very luxurious and comfortable means of transportation by comparison with what lay ahead. At that time, the railroad reached only the border of European Russia: from there they would have to travel by wagon or sleigh. At best—that is, if there were no extraordinary obstacles along the way—the trip would last two or three months. And who knows what awaited them upon arrival? But none of the three seemed to be thinking about that— all were tranquil and somehow exultantly joyful.

The unusual excitement Vera had experienced in the first days after her bold step had subsided, and she had again withdrawn into herself, becoming that quiet, dreamy, somewhat reticent young woman I first knew. She had lost some weight and looked older, but her dark-blue eyes continued to gaze cheerfully and boldly into the future, and it was exceedingly touching to see the tender care she lavished on her two companions, especially the older one. Evidently, all three were linked by a close friendship, a friendship that only common misfortune could secure.

Quite a crowd had gathered at the station. Some had come simply out of curiosity or sympathy, while others had relatives and friends in Siberia and wanted to send greetings or a bit of news with those departing. Naturally, the police were there in full force.

I barely managed to exchange a few words with Vera because of the crowd around her, but when the last bell sounded and the train was about to start, she extended her hand from the window to bid me farewell. At that moment, I could imagine so vividly the fate awaiting this charming young being that my heart grew heavy and tears rolled from my eyes.

"Are you crying for me?" said Vera with a bright smile. "Oh, if only you knew how much I, on the contrary, pity all of you who are staying here!"

Those were her last words.